The Cookie Crumbles
Copyright © 2017 Annie's.

The characters and events in this book are fictional, and any resemblance to actual persons or events is coincidental.

Library of Congress-in-Publication Data
The Cookie Crumbles / by Jan Fields
p. cm.
I. Title
                    2017938100

AnniesFiction.com
(800) 282-6643
Chocolate Shoppe Mysteries™
Series Creator: Shari Lohner
Series Editors: Janice Tate, Ken Tate
Cover Illustrator: Bonnie Leick

10 11 12 13 14 | Printed in China | 9 8 7 6 5 4 3 2 1

A pleasant breeze blew through the alley between the rows of storage buildings, almost making up for the fact that they were at a storage company on a Saturday afternoon. The breeze lifted a strand of Jillian Green's wild red hair and tossed it into her face. She pushed it aside and reached into the pocket of her light jacket, hoping to find a hair tie.

She did and quickly pulled her hair into the red poof that she preferred to think of as a ponytail. She made a mental note to set an appointment at the Clip & Curl. Now that the thick humidity of summer was over, the styling salon might actually be able to help get her red mane under control.

Jillian looked at the small crowd of people—altogether nearly two dozen of them—milling around the alley. Most wore casual clothes with sweaters and light jackets, though a few clearly refused to give up their summer T-shirts and short sleeves. In other words, a normal crowd for Moss Hollow, Georgia, in the fall. She picked up a general sense of excitement in the buzz of chatter about the pending auction.

Unlike the rest of the spectators, Jillian's Aunt Cornelia never left home in anything that might be considered casual. She was decked out in a neat floral skirt in shades of blue and a light wool jacket trimmed in tatted lace that Cornelia had made herself. The blue of the jacket perfectly matched the blue of Cornelia's eyes. Her short blonde curls were tucked under a white knit tam that perched on her head at a jaunty angle. The outfit and the excited sparkle in her eyes made Cornelia look much younger than her eighty years.

Turning her attention back to the milling crowd, Jillian was surprised that so many people would come out to bid on someone else's junk. She said as much to her great-aunt.

"You have to be kidding," Cornelia countered. "A storage unit auction is one of the world's biggest surprise packages. It's wonderful. Even people who don't want to own it will want to see it."

Jillian latched onto the most alarming part of Cornelia's remark. "Surprise package! You mean no one is going to show us what we're bidding on? Isn't there a much-loved saying about not buying a pig in a poke? We could end up with a truckload of rubbish to haul to the dump."

"Don't worry; we'll get a peek," Cornelia said. "Besides, I know what I'm bidding on. This first unit is the only one I'm interested in. It belonged to the Gonce family. They must have rented it before they left town about ten years ago. I ate at the Gonce Family Restaurant with your uncle several times, and they had the cutest decor. I'm certain that storage shed is full of things we can use to give the bakery a face-lift."

The Chocolate Shoppe Bakery looked fine the way it was, as far as Jillian was concerned. The customers liked the little bistro tables and chairs, even if they were beginning to look a little worn. "I don't know," Jillian said. "A lot of the people who come to the bakery have been coming for years. That sense of continuity is important to them, like visiting an old friend."

Cornelia gave her a withering look. "The chocolate éclairs and fresh bread are what's important to them. The decor is utilitarian."

"I enjoy the photos on the walls," Jillian said.

Her aunt waved away her weak protest. "Even Bertie admitted the customer area could use some updating when I told her I was going to an auction to look at some items. Unlike you, my sister has faith in my decorating tastes."

I suspect your sister was trying to get you to stop bugging her, Jillian thought. Her grandmother wasn't one to spend much time thinking about decor in the bakery. She wanted it clean and functional and full of delicious things. Bertie's passion was in the baked goods themselves, and she was a master at creating them. Jillian helped out as much as she could and her baking skills were definitely improving, but she doubted she'd ever match Bertie. But then, few could.

Bertie Harper and Cornelia Montgomery were twin sisters who definitely proved that people who looked alike could be very, very different. Cornelia was always brimming with cheer and imagination. She loved working on the garden and fussing over her clothes.

Bertie viewed her own looks the same way she viewed the bakery decor. Everything in her wardrobe screamed practicality and ease of movement. Bertie favored classics because that way she didn't have to replace them. The only time Jillian had ever seen her grandmother show interest in decorating was her commitment to maintaining Belle Haven as best she could. But even that was mostly from Bertie's unflagging sense of responsibility. Her grandmother felt they were duty bound to protect the history tied up in the estate.

Jillian thought herself a mix of both women, with much of the level-headedness of Bertie, but not quite as much stubborn single-mindedness.

She crossed her arms over her chest, wondering if she should have picked a warmer jacket or at least worn a sweater under her jacket. She'd thought her silk T-shirt would be enough. November in Georgia was far from chilly, but the alley between the rows of storage units was acting as a breezeway. She snuck a glance at a tall man nearby in a black T-shirt and wondered how he was able to stand there without shivering.

At least she'd warm up when they started carrying dusty old junk to the bakery van. "I wish Savannah could have come to lend a hand hauling whatever you buy. I know she would have if she hadn't been tied up in a meeting with a client."

"That girl sure has a keen work ethic," Cornelia said approvingly. "I'm glad y'all made up and are friends. She's a good person."

Jillian rolled her eyes. "I was hardly going to keep holding a grudge after twenty years. Besides, I understand her motivation." Jillian didn't really want to talk about her own part in the fight she'd had with Savannah so many years before. She was glad it was all behind them. She couldn't imagine navigating the social complexities of life in Moss Hollow without Savannah Cantrell to help. "We could sure use her work ethic here today. I think I'm getting muscle spasms in my back from thinking about all the carrying."

Cornelia flapped a hand in the air. "Don't worry about it. I knew this would be too much for you and me. I have that covered, and here he is now." She waved at someone over Jillian's shoulder.

Jillian turned to see Hunter Greyson striding toward them. Tall and lean, he'd eschewed his usual neatly tailored suit for a pair of blue jeans and a faded flannel shirt. Somehow he managed to make the extremely casual clothes look classy. Jillian had to admit, he looked really good, especially when he smiled and waved back at Cornelia.

Jillian plastered a smile on her face to cover up her surprise, while speaking out the side of her mouth. "Why didn't you tell me you'd called Hunter?"

"Because you can be such a ninny over anything to do with him," her aunt whispered back.

I am certainly not a ninny. Jillian admitted she was a little gun-shy when it came to men, especially blindingly handsome men, but that was excusable considering her former fiancé had turned out to be an embezzler. Plus, Aunt Cornelia and Bertie had thrown Jillian at Hunter from the moment she returned to Moss Hollow.

Hunter reached them and clapped his hands together as he looked over the crowd. "I'm glad I got here before the action started. I do love a good auction. You can find lots of interesting things. At least half the art in my house came from auctions." Though technically a local boy, Hunter had spent years away from Moss Hollow, only coming back when his family needed him to take over the Greyson and Sons Funeral Home. Somewhere along the way, he'd lost most of the thick local accent and spoke with only a slight drawl. Just enough to be completely charming.

"I'm surprised you could get away from work," Jillian said.

Hunter smiled down at her. "That's the beauty of hiring good help. You can sneak away now and then, confident that they can handle whatever comes along. Of course, it helps that we don't have any viewings or services scheduled for today."

Jillian nodded but had no real answer to that. She liked Hunter. It was hard not to. And when he smiled at her, it practically took her breath away. But the fact that he ran a funeral home could creep her out a little if she thought about it too long. She noticed he was looking at her as if the conversational ball was now in her court and her babble mode kicked in. "I wish someone would convince Bertie that business can be left in someone else's hands once in a while. She works entirely too hard. Of course, I'm probably not as much help as she needs."

"Oh pshaw," Cornelia chimed in helpfully. "You do fine. You haven't burned anything or set fire to the bakery in weeks."

Jillian winced. "Months, actually." *Thanks for bringing that up.*

"Well, Bertie certainly wouldn't have been willing to come anyway," Cornelia said. "Not for this particular unit."

Jillian looked at her aunt in surprise, and opened her mouth to ask why not, but Cornelia began waving the flyer she clutched about the auction and pointing. "Oh, look, I believe that's the new owner."

"New owner?" Jillian echoed.

Cornelia nodded. "These units were put in by Lemuel Flagg years ago when you were off in California. I went to school with Lemuel's older brother, so I know enough to be sure the business must be in better hands now. Those Flagg boys were both wild as March hares."

"Oh, in what way?" Curiosity piqued Jillian's mood. Two mysterious statements in less than two minutes. *Finally something interesting about the day.* But before Cornelia could answer, the stranger she'd pointed out set a wooden box on the ground near one of the storage unit doors. He stepped up on it and greeted the waiting crowd.

"I'm glad to see so many turn out for our first auction." The man was short and stocky with wide shoulders and a square face. Jillian suspected she could probably look at the man eye to eye without his box. He had an abundance of black curls, a dark shadow of beard, and thick horn-rimmed glasses. He also had a pronounced accent that Jillian knew had come from somewhere well north of the Mason-Dixon Line. "I'm Robert Skiff, owner of No Holds Barred Storage. We've got three units for auction today. I want to assure anyone with belongings in No Holds Barred Storage that we do not auction off units until the owners are deeply in default of payment. And even then we give owners repeated warnings before moving on to this step. Here at No Holds Barred Storage, we treat your stuff the way we'd treat our own."

He paused as if he thought there might be applause, but the crowd only stirred with anticipation. A fleeting look of disappointment crossed the man's face. "We're going to start with this unit." He pointed behind him with his thumb. "I'll open the unit door for a five-minute peek. Bidders and spectators may not enter the unit. You can only look at items from the outside. This unit contains furniture and miscellaneous items from a small local restaurant."

"That's the one," Cornelia whispered.

Yeah, I figured. Jillian gasped as the man pulled the storage door up and the crowd surged forward, pushing Jillian along with it. Apparently folks were really interested in looking over the units.

The storage unit was almost a wall of goods, with the majority of items not visible from the outside.

"Oh, oh, I see the cutest tables and chairs in there," Cornelia said, bobbing up and down beside Jillian to catch peeks between the crowd. Jillian caught glimpses, but she also caught someone's elbow in her ribs and a hard nudge from behind.

Hunter stepped closer and blocked the press of the crowd from behind Jillian and Cornelia, but even he could only do so much. After they looked for a while, Jillian pulled Cornelia back out of the throng. "We've seen enough. Do you still want to bid on it?"

"More than ever," Cornelia said. "The tables and chairs alone would be great to spruce up the bakery."

"Aren't they a little large?" Jillian asked. "The customer area in the bakery isn't exactly spacious, and Bertie won't thank you if you crowd it with furniture."

"Gracie Mae had small tables too. I'm sure they're in there."

"Gracie Mae?" Hunter echoed.

"Gracie Mae Gonce. She and her husband, Wallace, ran the Gonce Family Restaurant out near the highway. They closed it up suddenly and left town about ten years ago. No one knows why. The little country restaurant did a great business. I know it was packed every time I went in there, though admittedly that wasn't very often. I always figured the Gonces' marriage problems finally led to closing the business."

"They didn't get along?" Jillian asked.

Cornelia suddenly looked uncomfortable, as if she was sorry to have chosen the topic. "It was a long time ago." She turned away from them, gazing over the crowd. "Do you suppose all of these people will be bidding against me? I only have so much money. I'd hoped to get the contents at a bargain."

"I expect most of the folks are probably rubberneckers," Jillian said. Moss Hollow wasn't exactly a social whirl and it didn't take much to get people to show up for something if it promised an opportunity for distraction.

Skiff waved people back from the front of the storage unit and began the auction. It quickly became obvious that Jillian's assessment of the crowd was correct as very few of them joined in the bidding and most who did dropped out quickly. Soon only Cornelia and one other person were bidding.

"I hope he stops soon," Cornelia said fretfully. "I'm almost to my limit."

"Bid as long as you want," Hunter said. "I'll make up the difference. If the unit is as good as you say, I'm sure there'll be several things I can use."

Cornelia gave him a bright smile and a pat on the arm.

Jillian shifted in line to get a better look at Cornelia's competition. He was a handsome older man; she'd guess him to be in his middle sixties. He wore a light tan sweater and slightly darker slacks. He didn't look at all like someone who would be interested in quirky restaurant decor, but he did look familiar somehow. She pondered it for a moment, then pulled out her phone to take his photo. She'd show it to Bertie and Lenora later. Lenora Ryan, a large, jovial African-American woman, had worked with Bertie at the bakery for many years. Between them, they knew virtually every person in Moss Hollow.

The man turned to look at her as she held up her phone to snap the photo. She froze at the play of emotions on the man's face. His eyes widened, then narrowed as a look of outrage flashed over his face, and he ducked away so quickly that the photo was spoiled by the rapid movement. He slipped back into the crowd and Jillian couldn't see him. She shifted position a couple of times, but the man didn't come into view again.

Aunt Cornelia made another bid, her hand fretfully resting on her cheek. No one bid against her. "Oh, I was so worried that I wouldn't win," she said. "I'm glad that man decided he didn't want it."

"Yes," Jillian said distracted. "A good thing." But she doubted he'd quit bidding because he didn't want the unit. Somehow Jillian had alarmed him, and he'd left as a result.

"Jillian? Is something wrong?" Hunter asked.

She pulled her attention back to the present moment. "I'm not sure." She told him about the man's reaction to her trying to take his photo.

"Perhaps he's a private person," Hunter said. "Some people seem to be terrified of the loss of privacy in our social media age."

Jillian forced a smile. "You're probably right, though he seemed to really want the storage unit."

"Perhaps he reached his limit and it was simply coincidental that you tried to take his photo at that point," Hunter said.

Coincidences always made Jillian suspicious, but she simply nodded in response to Hunter's words. "You're probably right."

Her aunt patted her on the shoulder. "Well, if he is so photo phobic that he ran away, that means you helped me win the auction, so it all turned out wonderfully. Now let's see what's in that unit!"

Jillian followed Cornelia's bouncy gait, trying to feel the same optimism, but something about the man's shocked, outraged face as he ducked away left her feeling uneasy. She found herself hoping she wouldn't have to see that face again.

After they signed the papers and Cornelia handed over her

money, Robert Skiff turned the unit's contents over to them. "Remember, I'm not responsible for anything you find in there," he warned before leading the rest of the crowd off to the next unit up for bid.

"*That* was ominous," Jillian muttered.

The storage unit was piled floor to ceiling in some places and offered no path through the boxes, furniture, and assorted weird things. Jillian picked a taxidermy weasel from a collection of rather moth-eaten companions. "What are we going to do with all this junk?" she said. "Even with the bakery van, there is no way we'll be able to cart away a quarter of the stuff in this unit."

"It's exciting, isn't it?" Cornelia asked, her eyes shining. "I feel as if I'm going to stumble upon a treasure at any moment."

Jillian set the weasel on top of a stack of chairs. "I feel as though I'm going to stumble upon something horrible at any moment. We'll be making trips all day. And if we haul all this to the bakery, Bertie will kill both of us."

Cornelia rolled her eyes in an impressive imitation of a put-upon teenager. "Of course we won't haul all of it to the bakery. We only need to take the things I'm sure we'll use there. Everything else goes back to Belle Haven."

Jillian groaned. "Belle Haven? You haven't noticed how packed the third floor storage already is?"

"We'll manage. Anything that doesn't fit on the third floor can always be stored in the garage."

"The garage where Bertie parks the bakery van?" Jillian said. "Good luck with getting her to agree to that."

"I'll handle it," her aunt scolded. "Now hush so I can concentrate on sorting all these treasures out."

Jillian hushed, slumping against the nearest stable piece of furniture. The weasel eyed her balefully from his perch on the stack of chairs.

"You won't need to make as many trips as you think," Hunter said. "I didn't drive my car. I brought a larger vehicle from work."

Jillian looked at him in horror. "A hearse?"

Hunter burst out laughing. "No, I wouldn't use a hearse as a moving van. Grayson & Sons actually owns a large truck. You'd be amazed at how much furniture and other things you need to haul around when you own a funeral parlor. People expect a kind of quiet, understated elegance from a funeral home, so the furniture and carpet cannot be allowed to show wear. When my great-uncle was in charge, he felt having a full-time vehicle would save us a lot of money in moving fees. And he was right."

"Oh," Jillian felt her cheeks warm. "I'm sorry. Of course you wouldn't use a hearse. I think I'm getting some weird fumes from the pile of dead animals." She pointed at the collection of taxidermy creatures.

"They are a rather alarming group. Were all of these really used as decor in a restaurant? It seems unsanitary somehow."

"Actually Gracie Mae only had one out at a time," Cornelia said. "As I remember, she'd have events like 'Weasel Wednesday Specials' and 'Turkey Tuesday.' I remember my favorite was her Sunday special: 'You Otter Have Pancakes.' But we should probably take all the animals to Belle Haven. Bertie wouldn't care to have them at the bakery."

Jillian wasn't thrilled with the idea of a house full of preserved animals either, but she was beginning to realize the day would run smoother if she gave in to whatever Cornelia planned. Her aunt walked over and handed her a pink ceramic pig in a baby bonnet. "Here, put this in the bakery pile."

Jillian looked at the pig. "Really?"

"We can put it in the front window," Cornelia said. "It's cute."

Deciding that she would let Cornelia fight that one out with her sister, Jillian carried the pig to the front of the unit and set it down. "Since the crowd has moved on to a different row for the rest of the auctions, I think I can pull the bakery van closer to the unit. I'll go get it."

"Good idea," Cornelia sang out.

When Jillian pulled up to the storage unit and hopped out, she saw Savannah Cantrell strolling toward her. Her friend's long brown bob whipped around in the breeze. "I hope I didn't miss all the fun."

"I thought you had a meeting," Jillian said.

Savannah winked at her. "You'd be surprised at how fast I can move them along when I'm missing something."

"If by fun, you mean sorting through some truly strange things based on my aunt's definition of cute then, nope, you haven't missed it all."

Savannah shoved her hands in the pockets of her corduroy slacks and rocked on her toes. "Sounds like fun to me. I love strange."

"Which explains your attachment to my family." Jillian led the way back into the unit. She saw Cornelia unrolling what appeared to be a large sheet of leather and laying it on top of a pile of boxes. "What's that?"

"I'm not sure." Cornelia stared down at the uneven sheet of leather. "But I think it's a map."

Shoving strands of hair behind her ear, Savannah stepped up closer to Cornelia and studied the lines on the leather for a moment. Then she pointed. "I think you're right. That right there is Massey Creek. Look at the way it makes this weird loop here. When I was a kid I used to go swimming in that spot. And this up here . . ." Her finger slid further up the map. "I think that's over near the Johnson farm."

"Why would anyone make a map on an old piece of leather?"

"Maybe the map is incidental." Hunter fingered the edge of the leather. "From the feel of it, this is deer hide. Considering the abundance of stuffed animals, maybe this deer hide was used as decoration in the restaurant, the same as the rest."

"But someone drew on the leather with marker," Jillian said. "She flipped over a part of the hide where the map marks were especially dark. "Look at this, the ink soaked through. Whoever wrote this ruined the leather. You wouldn't hang this side up with those ink splotches. And what's this along the edge? I thought it might be more marker stain, but it feels hard."

Savannah touched the edge. "Maybe something spilled on it?"

""Forget the stain," Cornelia insisted. "I think this is a treasure map."

"Treasure?" Savannah echoed. "Really? That would be cool, but it doesn't seem likely. Why would someone leave a treasure map in a storage unit and then abandon it?"

"I don't have answers to that, but look here." Cornelia pointed to a small circle near the section of creek at the center of the map. "That is clearly what the map was drawn to locate. It might not be an x, but I think it's a treasure."

"We could go track down that spot," Savannah said, her voice almost wobbly with excitement. "That would be exciting. A lot of that area is still wooded and unused. There's no telling what might be up there. Cornelia could even be right. It might be a treasure."

"Of course I'm right," the older woman said. "I have a sixth sense about these things. It runs in the family"

Jillian folded her arms across her chest. "In that case, my sixth sense is sending me a message as well. If Savannah is right and that spot is wooded and unused, I know exactly what's up there: snakes, ticks, and other things I tend to try to avoid."

Savannah smiled at her. "Where's your sense of adventure? Your time in California flatly ruined you, Jillian Green. Remember how much fun we had when we went out to the Okefenokee Swamp?"

"I remember I was almost eaten by an alligator," Jillian said. "I don't think there are any alligators in Massey Creek."

Jillian turned to Hunter who had stepped close enough to touch the edge of the map. He studied the stain intently. "What do you think?"

"I don't know what the map was made to reveal," he said hesitantly, "but I do think I might know what substance has stained this edge."

"Oh?" Jillian said, feeling unease at Hunter's odd tone." What would that be?"

He took a deep breath. "I don't mean to alarm anyone, but I'm fairly certain that's old dried blood."

Jillian looked at the wide swath of stain, including several marks that could be blurred fingerprints. If they were made in blood, it was clear the sheet of leather had come into contact with a lot of it. "Are you sure?"

"Not completely, of course. But as a coroner, I have come into contact with quite a bit of blood-soaked cloth. That looks like blood to me."

"Well, this is leather," Cornelia said. "So something living once wore it. I imagine it bled when the leather was removed."

"That's not how tanning works," Hunter said. "There is usually only a little blood around the fatal wound and no one would tan that part of the animal skin."

Cornelia flapped a hand at him. "Fine. Maybe Gracie Mae plopped some raw meat on this in the kitchen and it stained."

Jillian wrinkled her nose. "That doesn't say much for her sanitation at the restaurant."

"Maybe that's why they closed," Cornelia said pointedly. "You're losing sight of what's important here. This is a map."

"That's true," Jillian agreed. "Though I know I would be more comfortable if that stain wasn't human blood."

"I could test it," Hunter said. All eyes turned to him. "I am the coroner. I can certainly test blood to determine if it's human. If you don't mind my taking a small sample of this with me." He pulled a pocketknife from his jacket and gave Jillian a questioning look.

"Yes," she said. "Please do. I know I'll feel better once I know for sure."

As he cut off a small strip of the stained leather, Cornelia reached over and tapped on the circle location drawn on the map. "I still think we need to focus on the important part of this." Her smile stretched into a grin. "We found a treasure map!"

A treasure map stained with blood of unknown origin, Jillian thought as she looked at the dark leather and shuddered. *What exactly has Aunt Cornelia won in this auction?*

By the time they had emptied the storage unit and hauled everything to either the bakery or to Belle Haven, even Cornelia's boundless optimism seemed spent. When Jillian suggested they shove the last load of junk into her office instead of hauling it up to the third floor, it was proof of how exhausted everyone was. Even Hunter agreed to the plan.

Of course, what had seemed like a good idea at the time became a little less appealing later when Jillian had to scramble over boxes and piles to get to her desk. As she wedged herself in, she was glad she wasn't claustrophobic. Her years of working at the high energy, noisy advertising agency in California had given Jillian the ability to ignore nearly anything around her in order to concentrate on the task at hand, and she was soon caught up in research on her laptop.

While staring intently at the screen on her laptop, Jillian reached out for her mug of tea and put her hand down on something furry. She jumped, her hand toppling a pile of papers beside her to the floor. Then she realized the fluff under her hand was Possum's tail. After supper, the cat had trailed her to her office and darted through the door before she could close it. Now he seemed to be testing out strategic locations for glaring at the various stuffed animals sitting on boxes in the crowded room.

As she stroked the cat's head, Jillian realized she'd already gotten a little sniffly from breathing in the dust and funky smells, but the office was still the best place in the house for her to try to match the leather map to an actual spot around Moss Hollow. Jillian suspected Savannah had gone home to do the same thing since her friend had insisted on taking several photos of the unrolled map before she left.

Jillian sneezed and rubbed her nose. She'd have to finish soon while she could still breathe. Possum gave up glaring at the weasel perched on the closest stack of boxes and walked over to sprawl on Jillian's keyboard and bat at her chin. "Do you mind?" she asked him.

Apparently he didn't since he rolled over and looked coyly at her.

Jillian assumed it was all those animals perched on every available surface that had suddenly made her office Possum's favorite spot in the house. The cat normally stayed glued to Cornelia. Jillian's great-aunt was convinced Possum's devotion was proof that he housed the spirit of Cornelia's late husband. Jillian was more inclined to agree with Bertie. Cornelia had simply bought the cat's affection with the sneaky application of bits of bacon.

"You're adorable," she told the cat as she gave him a poke, "but I'm trying to work." The cat seemed to go boneless as she pushed, requiring maximum effort to scoot him completely clear of the keyboard. As soon as she could see the screen again, she realized Possum's sprawl had locked up the computer. She sighed and rebooted. "Shouldn't you be guarding me from all these dead animals?"

As if he could hear her, Possum stood and swept his fluffy tail over her face before stalking back to the corner of the desk to return to his stare-down competition with the weasel. Jillian was pretty sure the weasel would win.

Jillian sneezed again. Maybe they shouldn't have given up so soon on carting this stuff upstairs. She hoped she wasn't giving herself some fatal infection from breathing mold. Then she pushed the thought away. If the work she'd done around Belle Haven hadn't killed her yet, she must surely be made of the hearty stock her grandmother always claimed.

The computer finished rebooting and Jillian called up the Web browser to look again at maps of the area. She'd already realized that Savannah's first assessment was surely right. The snaking line on the map was Massey Creek. It matched the meandering path of the creek on the maps she found online almost perfectly, suggesting that whoever had drawn the map had known the area well. Massey Creek was interesting. Sometimes it divided for a short distance into shallow streams, while other times the streams came back together into a wide, deep rush of water that looked more like a river than a creek. As far as Jillian could tell, the mark on the map was near one of the deepest sections.

She glanced away from the computer to look for a scrap of paper to write down the coordinates on the map that seemed to coincide best with the circle spot. She opened one of the boxes and found a menu from the Gonces' restaurant, with a piece of paper stuck protruding from it. Pulling the paper loose, she read a cryptic note: *If something bad happens remember Weasel Wednesday.* Jillian wondered what on earth that meant, but not for long. She turned the paper over and noted the coordinates for the marker on the map.

That's when Jillian noticed Possum's staring contest with the weasel seemed to be over. Instead the cat was looking sharply at the office's one window. The window opened onto Belle Haven's front veranda, but all Jillian could see through the window was darkness.

"Do you hear a critter outside?" Jillian asked. *I hope it's not a skunk.* A family of skunks had briefly taken up residence under the garden shed, and Jillian would prefer not to enjoy that odor quiet so regularly again.

The cat stood slowly, his tail lashing. Now his attention turned to the office door. The cat's fixed stare sent a cold chill up Jillian's back. *What is it with cats? Nothing on earth is creepier than a cat when it stares at nothing.*

Possum jumped off the desk and ran to the door. Normally a vocal creature, Possum was uncharacteristically silent as he sniffed at the base of the door, then looked pointedly back at Jillian. "I'll let you out of the office," Jillian said as she squeezed through the piles of boxes and odd bric-a-brac, "but I'm not letting you outside. It's too late. I don't want to walk around in the dark hunting you at bedtime, and I definitely don't want you getting mixed up with a skunk."

She opened the office door at the same exact moment someone turned the knob on the front door in the foyer. Since Jillian knew her grandmother and aunt were both upstairs, she froze, holding her breath as the door swung slowly open. A stranger stepped into the foyer, lit only by the moonlight behind him and the spill of light coming from the office behind Jillian.

The stranger turned toward the light and froze. For an instant, Jillian and the stranger locked eyes. His dark eyes were all Jillian could see as the man wore a ski mask and gloves, both items being unnecessary for the mild chill of the November night.

The only one who had kept moving through this was Possum. He raced across the foyer, leapt up on one of the plinths Cornelia often used to hold urns of flowers from the garden, and then jumped on top of the intruder.

Possum's needle-sharp claws sunk through the ski mask easily and broke the frozen moment. The man bellowed curses and batted at the cat on his head, stumbling out the front door as he did so. Jillian raced for the front foyer lights, shoving her hand in her pants' pocket as she ran, intending to pull out her phone and call the police. She quickly found her pocket empty and remembered that she'd left her phone on the desk because it was uncomfortable to sit on it. *Fine, I'll call the police after I get the lights on.*

She swept her hand over the row of switches, flipping on the foyer lights and the outdoor lights at once. Outside, she caught sight of the back of the fleeing man with Possum still riding on his head and shoulders. The man twisted and smacked at the cat, but Possum's ability to dodge the flailing hands seemed almost supernatural.

"Possum!" Jillian yelled, worried that the cat's luck would run out, and the intruder would hurt him.

Just as the man reached the shadows of the front garden, Possum jumped from his head. The man kept running, and Jillian could hear his heavy footsteps in the darkness, clearly moving away from her. The cat trotted back toward Jillian, his tail in the air and his gait jaunty. "Don't be so full of yourself," Jillian scolded. "He could have hurt you." Still, she was grateful for Possum's intervention, since the man might have hurt *her* if he'd stayed in the house.

As the cat closed the distance between them, Jillian heard a car engine start up in the distance and hoped it was the intruder leaving. As soon as Possum stepped through the door, Jillian closed and locked it. She leaned against the heavy door for a moment and wondered if it was worthwhile to call the police. She hadn't seen the man's face, and he'd been wearing gloves so there would be no prints. She had no idea what he was driving or even what he'd come to do. He hadn't been inside long enough to steal anything. And placing the call would mean it might be hours before she got to bed. For a moment, she weighed the possibility of his coming back, but suddenly she was simply too tired to face the idea of dealing with Moss Hollow's sometimes skeptical sheriff's department.

"Come on with me to the kitchen while I lock up," she told the cat. "I'll give you a treat for your bravery. I happen to know there are some leftover chicken livers in the fridge."

Though she knew the cat couldn't have understood her, he seemed to be in favor of joining her in the walk to the kitchen.

After giving him a piece of liver, Jillian had made up her mind. "I'm going to take a page from *Gone with the Wind*," she told Possum as he looked up at her. "I'll think about it tomorrow."

She walked through the house, carefully locking all the doors and checking the locks on the downstairs windows as well. It was a solid house with strong locks. Besides, it seemed unlikely the man would come back after his encounter with Possum. From what she'd seen, the man had to be hurting.

Though she felt more and more convinced that they were safe for the night, Jillian scooped up the cat and carried him upstairs to her room. She simply needed the warm, fluffy security of having an attack cat beside her.

Sunday dawned unusually bright, or so it seemed to Jillian when she woke to Possum patting her on the nose. She opened her eyes, wincing against the morning light coming in through the window. Usually she enjoyed waking up to the light, especially since working at a bakery meant getting up well before sunrise on weekdays, but today the sun pierced her head like an awl. With a groan, she sat up with her eyes closed tightly and rubbed the back of her neck. She'd slept poorly, chased through the night by villains in ski masks and by giant stuffed weasels.

Possum hopped off the bed and raced to the bedroom door, meowing plaintively.

"I know, I know," Jillian muttered as she felt around the floor with her toes, looking for her slippers. "You smell bacon."

Bertie could be counted on for bacon on Sunday, and Possum could track bacon better than a bloodhound. Jillian shuffled over and opened the door. As soon as the cat darted out, she trudged off to get a shower, hoping it would wake her up enough to get through the day.

By the time she got to church with Bertie and Cornelia, Jillian was well fortified with bacon and eggs and felt almost normal again, though not quite normal enough for casual conversation. She knew she needed to tell her grandmother and great-aunt about the near break-in, though in the light of morning, the whole incident seemed almost like something she'd dreamed up. In Moss Hollow, people felt comfortable with unlocked doors because it was usually such a safe place, not someplace where people in ski masks broke into homes.

"I hope you're not going to grunt your way through the Sweetie Pie meeting later," Bertie scolded. The Southern Sweetie Pies were members of a baking club led by Bertie that met in The Chocolate Shoppe each Sunday afternoon. "And if Pastor Keith speaks to you, I expect you to be gracious."

"Did I grunt?" Jillian considered reminding her grandmother that she wasn't a kid anymore and knew how to behave, but the thought required too much effort to vocalize and she settled for what she hoped was a fairly agreeable grunt.

The Sunday service was excellent as usual with a thought-provoking sermon about family, but Jillian had to concentrate to follow Pastor Keith's line of thought. She suspected the fault lay in her lack of sleep, not his homiletic abilities. Twice she caught herself drifting off and once Bertie gave her an elbow in the ribs and a stern glare, making Jillian suspect she might have snored.

"What is wrong with you?" Bertie demanded in a fierce whisper when the service ended and everyone rose to begin the meet, greet, and gossip portion of the Sunday tradition.

"I didn't sleep well," Jillian whispered back. "I'll tell you about it later."

"You certainly will."

In an effort to put off her grandmother's grilling, Jillian slipped away during the handshaking time and found Savannah gathering her things from her usual pew near the front of the church. Jillian felt mildly vindicated when she saw soft shadows under her friend's eyes. "Up late?" she asked.

Savannah laughed softly. "Of course. This is my first treasure map."

"You'll be so disappointed if that turns out to be a map to someone's favorite fishing hole." Though she teased her friend, Jillian begrudgingly felt a thrill at the idea of treasure.

She quickly accepted when Savannah invited Jillian to join her for lunch before the weekly Sweetie Pies meeting. Jillian was feeling less like a mercy member of the club since her baking skills were improving, but regardless, Bertie hosted the group at the bakery so attendance was mandatory. And the snacks were always excellent.

Jillian caught her grandmother's arm to let her know she was going to lunch with Savannah. Bertie gave her a stern look. "All right, but we'll still have that talk later."

And I'm so looking forward to it. Jillian walked out to Savannah's car. She had left her Prius at Belle Haven and had ridden to church in Aunt Cornelia's restored powder-blue Mustang fastback, a car Cornelia babied as much as she did Possum and for much the same reason: her late husband. The Mustang had belonged to Uncle Raymond, who'd loved it dearly, so Cornelia gave it good care in his honor.

Once they were in Savannah's car, Jillian leaned back against the headrest and closed her eyes. "Poke me if I fall asleep."

"I *thought* you weren't as blasé about the map as you pretended," Savannah said. "You spent the evening studying it too, didn't you? I must have compared the image to a half dozen maps online."

"At least you were probably in pleasant surroundings," Jillian said. "I was in my office surrounded by dead animals all trying to stare me down. And that was actually the best part of the evening."

Savannah gave her a sideways glance. "And the worst part?"

Jillian sighed and sat up straight. "Someone tried to break into the house. Actually, it didn't require a lot of breaking. I hadn't locked up yet, but since the man wore a ski mask and gloves, I don't think he was popping by for a visit."

Savannah gasped. "What did you do?"

"I have to say, it wasn't my finest moment. I mostly stared in shock," Jillian admitted. "It was Possum who took care of the guy. He jumped on the man's head and rode him right out into the yard. I'm betting the guy ended up with some serious scratches and bite marks under that mask."

"So he fled?"

"Yeah, and I locked up and went to bed, but I had a tough time sleeping after that."

"No surprise there." Savannah drove without speaking for a moment. "I don't suppose you called the police."

"Are you kidding? I figured the odds were in favor of Gooder showing up, and I didn't have the energy." Deputy Goodman "Gooder" Jones treated Jillian exactly like a particularly annoying sibling, so encounters with him took a lot of energy and self-control or they quickly descended into arguments. "The intruder didn't steal or break anything. Plus with gloves and a ski mask, I don't suppose he left much evidence either."

"Still, it's an attempted robbery." She paused again. "And there might be footprints. On TV the police figure out all kinds of things from footprints."

"There are a lot of things on cop shows that don't seem to happen in Moss Hollow," Jillian said.

"Do you think the break-in might be related to the treasure map?"

Jillian shrugged. "I didn't really think much about it last night. In California, I would have chalked it up to burglars, but Moss Haven isn't exactly a hotbed of crime. It's entirely possible someone could be after the map or something else mixed up in all the junk we took out of the storage unit. After all, someone thought the contents of the storage unit were valuable enough to bid hard against Cornelia."

"But she won," Savannah said.

"Only because the other bidder ran off when I tried to take his picture."

"Why would you take his picture?"

"I don't know really. I guess he was so intent on winning the auction and he looked familiar. I figured I'd show it to someone who knew more people in Moss Hollow and find out the man's name."

"Did you get the picture? I could take a look at it. I know a lot of people."

Jillian slumped back against the headrest again. "Yeah, I have the picture on my phone but it's too blurry to be very helpful. And before you ask the next question, I don't have a clue if the bidder was the same person who tried to break in last night. It might have been, since they were both average size."

"So is this encounter the reason Bertie was giving you the stink eye?"

Jillian shook her head, then shrugged. "Not exactly. She doesn't know about the break-in, but Bertie can smell a secret from a mile away. I'll have to tell her about it."

"And you should. If someone tries to break into Belle Haven again, everyone needs to know about it."

Jillian held up a hand. "I know, I know. I didn't have the energy to go into it before church."

"Well, rest your eyes, and I won't make you talk until we get to my house."

Savannah was as good as her word, and Jillian enjoyed the rest of the ride. When she felt the car slow to a stop and the engine turn off, she opened her eyes. Savannah's small bungalow looked as cheerful as ever with its light yellow siding and bright white trim. Though Belle Haven could practically eat the little house as a light snack, there was something enchanting and homey about the cozy little house.

As soon as Savannah opened the door, the savory smell of soup filled the air.

"I smell lunch." Jillian slipped out of her light jacket and hung it on the old-fashioned coatrack near the door.

"I love slow cookers," her friend answered. "It's like coming home to someone having cooked for you."

The soup turned out to be a wonderful blend of tomatoes, Italian sausage, cannellini beans, and onion in a rich broth. Savannah stirred in a small bag of frozen tortellini. "We'll give them a few minutes to cook," she said. "And that will give me time to toast some bread."

"Is there anything I can do to help?" Jillian asked, though Savannah's small kitchen didn't really work well with two chefs.

"You could set the table, if you don't mind."

As she set out the lovely stoneware dishes, Jillian thought of how the little house looked roomier than it was because Savannah allowed no clutter at all. The result should have been severe but the harmonious color choices, warm wood floors, and beautiful fabrics in the drapes and chair cushions made it simple but homey.

When they were finally sipping soup, Savannah gave Jillian a sly grin. "I was up late last night too, as you know."

Jillian straightened her spine. "I know that look. You figured it out, didn't you? In my defense, I think I came close before the whole breaking and entering thing. I managed to confirm that is Massey Creek on the map and then I found a note with coordinates that I'm pretty sure match the spot on the map." She pulled the note from her purse and showed Savannah the numbers scrawled on the back.

"I did pretty well." Savannah's smile looked a bit smug. "Those match the numbers I came up with almost perfectly. In fact, I loaded my phone with the GPS coordinates I came up with, but I can tweak it to match those."

Jillian widened her eyes. "Well, if we didn't have a Sweetie Pies meeting, I'd say we should sneak off to find the spot. But if I ditch the meeting, Bertie will have my hide."

"I figured we could go after the meeting," Savannah said. "It's going to be a bit of a hike, but I think you probably need to tell Bertie and Cornelia about it. After all, technically, it's Cornelia's map. And you should probably tell them about the break-in as well."

Jillian sighed. "I suppose."

Savannah finished altering the coordinates in her phone and handed the crumpled note back to Jillian, who stuffed it back in her purse. Savannah must have seen the gloom on Jillian's face because she promptly changed the subject, asking Jillian about her baking progress. Jillian had good news on that front. She had actually tackled croissants.

Savannah paused in the middle of sipping from her glass of sweet tea. "Croissants? Wow, I'm not sure I could do those justice."

"I didn't say I did them justice. But I didn't set a fire, so I consider it a win."

"Well, it wouldn't be a loss."

Conversation continued as they compared bread-making techniques, something Jillian was amazed to be able to converse about intelligently. She certainly was changing as she worked at the bakery, which was good. The whole purpose of her move back to Moss Hollow was to someday take over The Chocolate Shoppe, something that Bertie always reminded her about. After lunch, Jillian helped her friend with the dishes before they hopped back into Savannah's car to head to the Sweetie Pies meeting.

The Sweetie Pies had a nearly full turnout, missing only Annalise Reed who'd gone with her husband, Byron, on a romantic weekend getaway, a trip she'd talked about for weeks. Jillian was glad for Annalise, though she was a little jealous too. Jillian was happy. She had friends. Every day, she could see she was growing more competent at the bakery. And Moss Hollow rarely gave her a dull day. But for all that, she sometimes thought it would be nice to have someone who adored her the way Byron adored Annalise.

Shaking off the melancholy, Jillian forced her attention to the women around her. The baking club was a group as dedicated to gossip as goodies, but they certainly did goodies well.

Though Jillian would definitely identify Bertie as the best baker among them, there wasn't a person in the Sweetie Pies who couldn't hold her own in the kitchen, with the possible exception of Jillian.

The Sweetie Pies took turns bringing their favorite treats to the club meetings. This week, the Moss Hollow reference librarian, Josi Rosenschein, shyly passed around trays of pumpkin cookies, then seemed genuinely surprised when everyone raved over them.

"Do you mind if I bake up some of these for the bakery?" Bertie asked as she looked over the recipe cards Josi handed out. "I'm always getting requests for new pumpkin treats."

Josi beamed. "If you think they're good enough."

Savannah threw an arm around Josi. "You are going to have to learn how to blow your own horn if you're going hold your own in the Sweetie Pies. You're a truly fine baker."

"I do love baking," Josi said as her cheeks glowed pink.

Maudie Honeycutt, a septuagenarian with snow-white hair in a cute pixie cut, waved a cookie in the air. "Well, I think these are great. I believe I'll put some in my Christmas care packages for my grandkids. I try to send them lots of real Southern baking to make up for the tofu and kale lifestyle that surrounds them."

Maudie's best friend, Wanda Jean Maplewood, tut-tutted

at her remark. "I'm sure there are sane folks out there. After all, Jillian lived in California for twenty years, and it doesn't seem to have affected her."

Jillian heard her grandmother mutter something that sounded like "much," but she chose to ignore it as she carried her cookie over to a table. The Sweetie Pies launched into the month's business, which mostly amounted to deciding which charity functions to attend or provide baked goods for.

"We have to do the big Paws and Purrs bazaar," Maudie insisted. "We do baked goods for their treats table every year and the animal shelter needs that money."

"That'll be fine," Bertie agreed. "The bakery will donate a few dozen cupcakes decorated with paw prints, same as last year."

"The church will have a bazaar as well," Lenora reminded them. "And we ought to make some desserts for the Thanksgiving charity baskets. I don't mind baking a few extra pumpkin pies."

The chatter about charity bazaars threatened to pull Jillian back into her earlier lethargy, so she stood up to get a cup of coffee, hoping a caffeine jolt would keep her awake. She'd barely gotten back to the table when she realized no one was talking and they were all looking at her.

"What?"

"I think it's time you told us why you look like something Possum dragged in," Bertie said.

"You do look tired, dear," Cornelia added.

Savannah gave her a sympathetic smile but, since no one seemed to notice her own dark circles, did nothing to rescue her, so Jillian finally told the story of the near break-in. To her surprise, it wasn't Bertie who reacted the strongest.

"And you didn't think to call our office?" Laura Lee Zane asked. As the youngest sheriff's deputy in Moss Hollow, Laura Lee took her role as protector of the community very seriously.

Jillian repeated the excuses she'd given Savannah, but they sounded weaker every time she went through them. "Honestly, I don't know what y'all would have done. Nothing was stolen and Possum ran the man off."

"I would have made a report, for one thing," Laura Lee said. "If this is the beginning of a series of burglaries, we need a report of it. What if this guy was trying out his technique at Belle Haven last night before moving on to other homes?"

"Then I reckon Possum taught him a thing or two," Bertie said. She rarely praised the cat since he'd deserted her in favor of her sister, but clearly she was proud of his attack on the burglar.

Jillian noticed Laura Lee's frown never wavered as she looked at Jillian. Jillian held up both hands. "Fine, I'm reporting it now, though I doubt it's going to happen to anyone else. I have a suspicion this one was directed right at us."

"What?" Bertie demanded. "Have you annoyed someone new?"

Jillian gawked at her grandmother. "No, I haven't annoyed someone new. But someone bid vigorously against Aunt Cornelia on that storage unit, right up until the moment I tried to take his photo. Then he ran off. We found a mysterious map amongst the piles of junk in the storage unit, a map which may or may not point toward a treasure. And then someone tries to break in. I think it's all related."

Laura Lee eyed her skeptically. "Sometimes it's easy to see a pattern in coincidence. But can we detour for a moment to the whole treasure map thing. You found a treasure map?"

Jillian eyed the rapt expressions around her and settled in to tell her story of the auction and the map. Cornelia seemed to wake up to the conversation and threw in several remarks when she felt Jillian wasn't including enough details. It was Cornelia who made sure to mention Hunter helping them. "When I asked him to come, he practically couldn't say 'yes' fast enough."

"Good to hear," Maudie said. "It's about time Jillian and Hunter started dating good and proper."

"It wasn't a date," Jillian insisted. "He helped move furniture."

"My first date with Raymond was when he helped me weed the front flower beds," Cornelia said, her eyes dreamy. "It's amazing how much two people can bond over work."

About the time Jillian despaired of getting off the topic of Hunter, Laura Lee cleared her throat loudly. "Can we get back to the treasure map? Do you have any idea of where it leads?"

"I do," Savannah said, taking up the narrative. She pulled out her phone to show everyone a map with the spot marked. "I have the coordinates. As far as I can tell, it's about two miles into the woods above Johnson farm. I thought maybe we could go check it out after the meeting."

"I'm not sure who you mean by 'we,'" Maudie said. "But I want to say that I'm not hiking through the woods, especially not to follow some questionable map pulled from Gracie Mae Gonce's collection of junk. I don't remember her ever hanging up a map, but I do know that woman collected junk like a bee collects pollen."

Wanda Jean gave Maudie a disappointed look. It was obvious she would have liked to join the treasure hunt, but not without her best friend. "We will want to know exactly what you find out there," she said, tapping the table with one finger. "And don't make us wait for another Sweetie Pie meeting. You know how much I hate being left out."

Lenora, who had remained quite throughout the entire discussion of break-ins and treasure maps, crossed her arms over her ample bosom and gave Jillian a disapproving look. She was almost as good at disapproving looks as Bertie, but Jillian figured she'd probably learned it from Bertie while working at the bakery for over thirty years. "I don't think it's a good idea for anyone to hike out in the woods this time of year. It happens to be deer season, as you might remember."

"I agree with Lenora," Bertie said. "This is a dangerous time of year for wandering in the woods. And it's ridiculous to think Gracie Mae hid anything of value in that storage unit. The only thing you're going to find out in those woods is deer and deer hunters."

"I think we'll be perfectly safe if we take precautions," Laura Lee said. "I have a bunch of blaze orange vests in the back of my car from the last big litter pick up."

"Sounds good," Cornelia said. "I had the most extraordinary dream about the map last night. I'm certain we'll find something of great significance. I'm in."

"You most certainly are *not* in," Bertie snapped at her sister. "Stop being silly and remember your age."

Cornelia scowled at Bertie, but since everyone knew which of the sisters was more strong-willed, she finally slumped in sulky defeat. "Fine. But at least one of us should represent Belle Haven." She looked pointedly at Jillian.

Having been shot at more than once in the past, Jillian wasn't overly excited at the idea of going out in the woods during hunting season, but she certainly wasn't going to miss a chance to find out what the map was drawn up to show. "Of course I'll go."

Bertie didn't look happy, but she didn't say anything against the idea.

"Great, so it's Laura Lee, Jillian, and me," Savannah said, clapping her hands together. She turned to look at the quiet librarian beside her. "How about you, Josi? Want to go treasure hunting?"

Josi smiled but shook her head. "I would love to, but I can't. I have to do some organizing at the library this evening. I haven't had a spare minute during regular hours, which is good, but it's put me behind." Then she raised her hand. "But put me on the list of people who want to know what you find."

Savannah made an imaginary check mark in the air. "You're on it." She turned to grin at Jillian and Laura Lee. "This will be so much fun."

"Yeah," Jillian said, trying to sound enthusiastic but knowing she wasn't entirely successful. She wasn't sure why, but she had an ominous feeling of doom. Had she just signed up for something she was going to really, *really* regret?

The woods smelled of the end of summer, sharp and faintly musty. There was something about the stillness, the faintly alien feel of humans being far from other humans that made Jillian slink along as quietly as possible, but Laura Lee insisted they keep talking. "Blaze orange helps," she said, "but it's hard to confuse something for a deer when you hear a human voice. We're not trying to sneak up on the deer out here, so it's better for us to be noisy."

Both reasons made perfect sense, and yet Jillian still had trouble speaking at her normal volume, and she noticed Savannah did as well. Still, she made the effort. "So," she said, then cleared her throat and tried again. "So, ladies, how's work?"

Laura Lee chuckled. "The most interesting thing I've done at work lately is break up a fight in the parking lot of Crazy Fish, which is why I'm so excited by the map you found. I could really use an adventure."

"And the most interesting thing I've come across lately was a new tax break for one of my customers," Savannah said. "I'm with you, Laura Lee. I need a little excitement."

"Be careful what you wish for," Jillian said. "I sometimes find things around here too adventurous."

Laura Lee laughed. "According to Gooder, you make your own adventure."

Once again, Jillian thought of how Deputy Jones had become the bane of her existence since she'd come back to Georgia. Years ago they'd gone to school together, and so they had a kind of vague fondness borne of long acquaintance overlaid by Jillian's urge to pinch him about half the time when he smirked his way through any investigation that involved her. And there had been a lot of investigations involving her since she came home. "Gooder just enjoys complaining," Jillian said.

"He does at that," Laura Lee agreed cheerfully. "Especially about you."

Then, somewhere in the distance, they heard the sound of a rifle shot and Jillian's brief period of growing relaxation halted. She shifted the shovel she was carrying from one shoulder to the other and tried to come up with another conversation starter, but her head seemed to be full of nothing but fog and anxiety.

Then the sound of someone crashing through the woods came from somewhere in front of them. Laura Lee took a step forward and lifted her shovel from her shoulder. Though her stance looked casual at first glance, Jillian could see the tension in her shoulders and the careful way she positioned her feet for the best balance. Whatever was coming, Laura Lee clearly planned to be ready for it. Jillian copied the young deputy's stance as best she could. From the corner of her eye, she saw Savannah do the same.

The crashing sounds became louder. For a moment, Jillian wondered if they should all start shouting or something. If the noises were coming from a person, she didn't want to be mistaken for a deer and shot. Of course, the sounds might be from a bear. She tried to remember if they even had bears in this part of Georgia. It's not as if she spent a lot of time out here. Certainly Tennessee and North Carolina had bears. Did they have bears this far south? She realized she was doing a kind of mental babbling from the tension of waiting to see what was approaching and shook herself mentally.

Then, so quickly that it almost seemed to have magically appeared, a deer burst out of the woods in front of them. It was a doe, sturdy and plump from a summer of good eating. The doe froze for an instant at the sight of three women brandishing shovels, then changed direction slightly and bounded away into the woods again.

For a moment, all three of them held their frozen pose, then they collectively let out the breaths they'd been holding. "That deer nearly scared me to death," Savannah said with a giggle.

"I'll admit," Laura Lee said, "my adrenaline is definitely pumping."

Jillian realized hers was as well, since she couldn't feel a trace of the sleepiness that had dogged her up to that point. Instead, she pressed a hand to her chest as if to hold her pounding heart in place. "Well, you guys wanted this to be an adventure."

"True," Savannah said cheerfully. "And that deer was beautiful. I hope no one shoots her."

Laura Lee started off down the trail and the others followed. "I imagine someone already shot *at* her. That's probably what sent her crashing through the woods."

They trudged along for a while, and Jillian felt her pounding heart calm, though she remained more alert. She soon picked up on the sound of running water. "Is that Massey Creek?"

"Should be," Laura Lee said. "If it's the bend, that means we're not far from the spot on the map."

Savannah pulled out her phone and called up her GPS app. "It looks like we're on track." She pointed off in the direction Jillian had heard the water sounds. "The bend of the creek should be right over that way."

"Let's head for it," Laura Lee suggested. "And then walk back toward the circle from the creek. It might help us get a better sense of what makes that area special."

Jillian wasn't sure how that approach would be better, but she was agreeable enough. The sooner they found the spot they were searching for, the sooner they could get out of the creepy woods.

When they reached the bank, Jillian saw this was one of the wilder spots with the water practically roaring over the rocky creek bed far below. The banks were high and trees seemed to cling right to the edge, leaning toward the creek slightly as though curious about what lay below the raging water. Jillian knew erosion would eventually wear away the banks enough to send those trees toppling into the water, but until then, they shaded the roiling water below.

Savannah stood near the bank and slowly turned around, holding up her phone and watching the screen all the while. She pointed off through the trees. "The spot on the map is that way."

The woods around them grew sparser, but that only gave the undergrowth more room and light so their progress slowed as they pushed through brush. "At some point, this area must have been cleared land," Laura Lee said as she stomped down a briar. "Maybe a homestead."

Up ahead, Jillian could see that the land sloped steeply upward in a rocky hill. She had little interest in scrambling up the hillside, especially when she saw that more of the obnoxious briars grew on the hill, along with a tangle of thick vines bearing bright-red leaves that she was fairly certain was poison ivy.

Another lanky briar cane smacked against Jillian's jacket, making her glad for the fabric's weight. Otherwise, the briar would probably have drawn blood. For all the excitement she could hear in Laura Lee and Savannah's voices, she couldn't share it. She definitely did not want to climb the hill that rose up ahead of them, and she certainly wasn't seeing any signs of treasure.

She'd just shoved aside more clinging briars when her foot struck a rock and she pitched forward, right into a tangle of thorny canes. She managed to avoid scratching her face, but the thorns tangled in her ponytail, leaving her wallowing to get up while the briars seemed intent on pinning her to the ground by her hair. "Ouch! Ouch! Ouch!"

"Hold still," Laura Lee said as she moved closer through the brush. "I'll get you loose." She pulled a knife from her pocket and carefully cut the briar stems, then she and Savannah hauled Jillian to her feet.

"I'm not having as much fun as I'd hoped," Jillian said, then yelped as one of the thick briar thorns pierced her thumb as she tried to pluck the stem from her hair.

"Let us do it," Savannah suggested. "We can see how to avoid the thorns better."

"Okay, thanks." Jillian crossed her arms over her chest and tried not to whine as her friends carefully separated her hair from the cut stems. She couldn't avoid wincing, however, when their efforts required pulling.

As she stood there, her gaze swept the area to keep her mind off the pain. She saw there were more rocks, all partially hidden amongst the overgrowth. Lots more. And she could see they were actually piled in places. With a gasp she pointed at one spot where the pile of rocks made a clear right angle. "Look over there. I think this is an old foundation."

The tugging on her hair stopped. "I think you're right," Laura Lee said. She staggered on ahead through the mat of undergrowth.

"We're practically right on top of the spot on the map," Savannah said. "Assuming I calculated correctly."

Jillian reached up to feel for more briars in her hair. "So it might have been an old map to someone's homestead and not to a treasure."

"Maybe," Laura Lee said. "I hate to write it off too—hey!"

Jillian gasped as Laura Lee vanished. One moment she was stomping through the brush around the foundation and the next, she was gone. "Laura Lee!"

"I'm okay," her friend yelled. "I fell in a hole."

"A hole!" Excitement filled Savannah's voice as she scrambled after Laura Lee. "Do you see anything down there that might be treasure? A box or a trunk?"

"It's not that kind of hole."

Jillian carefully picked her way toward the hole. The glow of a flashlight beam shone up from it as she reached the edge. She could see how Laura Lee had missed seeing it. The undergrowth had grown so densely that it camouflaged the hole unless you knew it was there. It reminded her of the kinds of pit traps she'd seen in old adventure movies.

Suddenly Laura Lee thrust her hands up. "Pull me up, please. There's nothing down here but spiders and roots."

Jillian and Savannah each grabbed a hand and hauled their friend out of the hole. As they pulled, Jillian was glad of Laura Lee's slender frame. Finally they had her back on the surface. Jillian brushed at the dirt clinging to Laura's clothes, and Savannah pulled a wad of something out of the deputy's hair.

"Why is there a big hole here?" Savannah asked. "Do you think someone already got the treasure?"

"I doubt it," Laura Lee said as she wiped at her face with her dirty sleeve. "The hole looks natural. It's probably a sinkhole. This whole area is being undermined by springs and the water from the creek."

Jillian looked around in alarm. "Do you think it's dangerous here?"

"Too dangerous to build on," Laura Lee said. "But I think we're all right for now." She pulled off the blue bandana that she'd been using for a headband for her blonde hair and tied it to one of the plants growing near the hole. "Maybe we can help keep the hunters from falling in it."

Jillian looked around the old foundation and wondered if her friends were going to insist they dig around it looking for treasure. She couldn't figure out if that sounded better or worse than climbing the big hill nearby. She looked toward the hill and caught something she'd missed before. She wove through the undergrowth toward it.

"What?" Savannah said. "Did you see something?"

"The hill," Jillian said. "It's got a door."

Laura Lee and Savannah followed close on Jillian's heels to the hillside. Jillian pulled on the gloves she'd brought and began pulling on the vines and other growth covering the door to what was obviously a root cellar. Savannah and Laura Lee joined in, with the deputy hacking at some of the vines with her knife. Finally they had the door uncovered enough to haul it partway open. The darkness inside was absolute.

Laura Lee held out her flashlight toward Jillian and Savannah. "I was the one who fell in the sinkhole. It's someone else's turn to tangle with the spiders."

"When you put it that way," Jillian said as she took the flashlight, "who could resist?" She turned on the flashlight beam and squeezed into the crack.

"Do you see anything?" Savannah yelled. "Do you want me to come in?"

"It's not exactly roomy in here." Jillian swept the beam over the hard-packed dirt walls. Someone had pounded pegs into the dirt and set boards across them for shelves. The shelves held old jars. Some were broken, but many were whole, their contents completely obscured by dust and grime.

"Do you see anything valuable?" Savannah's voice vibrated with excitement.

"Not unless you enjoy really old preserves," Jillian yelled back. She turned the flashlight beam to the floor and spotted a pile of old rags and white sticks. *Have they stored old clothes in here?* Then her brain caught up with what her eyes were really seeing. The thing sprawled across the dirt floor was a skeleton dressed in rags. The treasure they'd found was death.

5

Jillian backed out of the dark root cellar as quickly as she could. Her head felt light, almost swimming, so she took a few steps past her friends and sat on a rock, leaning over so her head was close to her knees.

Jillian felt a hand on her shoulder and flinched. "Jillian," Savannah said. "What is it? What's in there?"

Jillian tried to answer but she had to take a couple more long breaths before her voice returned. She looked up. "A body. I think it's a woman, but it's hard to tell." She turned to look back toward the entrance to the root cellar. She didn't see Laura Lee. Apparently the deputy had gone in as quickly as Jillian had come out.

"A body?" Savannah echoed.

Jillian nodded. Their treasure hunt had certainly not turned out the way they'd hoped. Laura Lee stepped out of the root cellar, several shades paler than she went in, and fished her phone from her jacket pocket to call in their discovery to the sheriff's department. Then she looked at Jillian and Savannah as she traded her leather gloves for a pair of latex gloves she had pulled from her other jacket pocket. "You'll have to stay out of the root cellar until we process the scene."

"That works for me," Jillian said. "I don't need to see that again."

"Jillian said she thought it was a woman?" Savannah said.

Laura Lee nodded. "Judging by the clothes and the few bits of hair still on the skull, it appears to be a woman. The body is mostly skeletonized. I'm not a forensics expert by any means, but my guess is that the body has been in there for years."

Jillian wrapped her arms around herself, trying to calm the shakes going on inside. "So maybe the map was a murderer's keeping track?"

"I don't know."

"The stains on the map." Jillian's voice felt tight in her throat. "The ones Hunter found. He said they looked like blood, and he took a sample. I haven't heard back yet on what he learned from testing it. Do you suppose they could have come from that person in there?"

"Maybe," the young deputy said. "I'll have to take the map into evidence now. I'll find out if that test revealed the stains were human blood. If they were, we can commission a DNA test to compare the stains to the remains. We'll know then if they match. That might also help determine cause of death. I'm no coroner, but I certainly couldn't see any damage on those bones that suggested what might have killed her." Laura Lee held up her phone. "I'm going back in to shoot some photos. Y'all wait here for the rest of my team."

Jillian and Savannah nodded at the same time. *Like bobble-head dolls*, Jillian thought. She watched Laura Lee dart back through the door, and Jillian felt a swell of gratitude for the young woman's brisk efficiency. There was comfort in knowing someone knew how to handle such a grisly discovery.

"I can't believe a silly treasure hunt turned into this," Savannah said.

Again Jillian nodded without speaking, marveling at how numb she felt. This wasn't the first dead body she'd ever seen, but it certainly wasn't something she was getting used to.

"Do you think the body could be Gracie Mae Gonce?" Savannah asked.

Jillian considered the question. "I don't know. I never met the Gonces. I don't really know anything about them other than what

Aunt Cornelia said about them having a cute country restaurant."

Savannah gaped at her in surprise. "Really? I figured you knew all about the brouhaha between Bertie and Gracie Mae."

"What are you talking about?"

"You'll have to ask Bertie or Cornelia to get the full story, but I know Bertie was livid when Gracie Mae added a bakery to that country restaurant of hers. I don't think it pulled much business away from The Chocolate Shoppe, but it sure got Bertie worked up. I heard her rant about it more than once at Sweetie Pies meetings. And then when Gracie Mae joined the Sweetie Pies . . ." Savannah whistled low. "Good thing that didn't last."

"I didn't know any of that." Back when she was living in California, Jillian had always thought Bertie had told her everything about the goings on in Moss Hollow during their twice weekly phone chats. She'd certainly kept Jillian updated on good reasons to leave California and come back to Georgia. Jillian wondered if she might have tuned out details of a business feud. Maybe, especially if she'd thought it was Bertie trying to convince her to come home for the good of the family business.

Savannah reached out to pick a lingering piece of briar vine from Jillian's hair. "Honestly, I thought Bertie was going to pop a blood vessel when Gracie Mae started coming to the Sweetie Pies meetings."

"That must have been exciting."

"Chilly is closer to the truth. Even Maudie and Wanda Jean skipped a couple meetings to avoid the tension, and you know it's bad when they choose peace over potential gossip fodder."

"Gracie Mae couldn't have felt exactly welcome, especially if members stopped coming to avoid her. Why would she come to a meeting if she wasn't really wanted?"

"I don't know. My guess is that she enjoyed making Bertie crazy, though I don't know why. Apparently they'd known one another since they were kids. I never got the whole story. I have to admit, I skipped a few meetings myself."

"Why didn't someone tell Gracie Mae to stop coming?"

"Because we don't keep anyone out, as you know. We're not that kind of club. But every meeting was like nuclear winter with those two there. I truly believe it might have killed the club entirely if the Gonces hadn't up and left town. Everyone breathed easier after that."

"If they all did leave town." Jillian looked pointedly toward the root cellar door.

Savannah followed her gaze and visibly shuddered. Then they both jumped as the phone in Savannah's jacket pocket began blasting country music. "Sorry." Savannah fumbled the phone out of her pocket and looked at the screen. She gave Jillian an apologetic smile. "Work. I should take this."

Jillian nodded. She stood and walked carefully through the brush, trying to follow the trail they'd already partially stomped into the undergrowth. After hearing that Bertie and Gracie Mae had been in serious conflict, she fretted more and more. If those were Gracie Mae's remains, how quickly would the police look at Bertie as a suspect? How was it that these terrible situations kept popping up? Moss Hollow was supposed to be a nice, quiet town.

Her agitated wandering took her to the far edge of the clearing, and she looked into the woods beyond where the canopy of trees shaded the ground enough to keep down the briars and brush. As her gaze swept the spaces between trees, her attention was drawn sharply to movement, followed by a rustle in the fallen leaves.

It was far too soon for deputies to arrive in response to Laura Lee's call, and Jillian wondered if it might be another deer. She took a hesitant step into the woods, stepping around a thin tree to get a different angle. That's when she caught a glimpse of a pale face marred by long scratches.

The man's face turned to a scowl before he turned and ran through the trees. The brief glimpse was enough. Jillian recognized it as the same man who'd bid against Cornelia at the auction. And the scratches made it clear that he *was* the one who'd tried to break into Belle Haven as well.

"Hey!" Jillian called and ran after him. She crashed through the brush, dodging trees and rocks and roots as she ran. Unfortunately, the man was clearly a better runner in the woods and she soon lost sight of him. Panting from the exertion of the run, she leaned against the rough bark of a tree and fought to catch her breath.

As soon as she could breathe without wheezing, she turned around, looking for the way back to the root cellar. To her alarm, she realized the trees all looked exactly alike. She saw no sign of her passage through them, and suddenly she wasn't even sure she was facing in the right direction. She was lost.

She reached into her jacket to pull out her phone and call Savannah. Maybe her friend could figure out a way to track her or at least give her survival tips. Savannah had always been far fonder of nature than Jillian. Then she groaned aloud as her phone showed both no reception and almost no charge. In her upset the night before, she'd forgotten to charge it. "Great," she murmured. "Exactly perfect." How was she supposed to find her way out of the woods?

She tried to remember anything she'd ever heard about being lost in the woods. *Wasn't there something about moss on the sides of trees?* The trees around her seemed to have stuff growing all over them, so that wasn't helpful at all. She listened for the sound of running water. If she could find her way to the creek, she could follow it up to the bend. She was sure she could find her way to the root cellar from there.

She held her breath, listening so intently for the sound of water that it nearly hurt. When she did hear something, it wasn't water. It was the pop of a rifle shot and the sound of tree bark splintering within a few feet of her head.

Jillian threw herself to the ground. *Why are people always shooting at me?*

6

Jillian wriggled, hoping to burrow into the fallen leaves and become a less obvious target. With her heart in her throat, she waited for another gunshot, her skin crawling with the thought of the shooter aiming for her exposed back.

The shot never came. Instead, she heard crashing through the bushes. She wondered if the shooter had mistaken her dive. Did he think she was shot? Was he coming to finish the job? Should she play dead? She swallowed a whimper and slowly raised her head to look in the direction of the sounds.

A middle-aged man in jeans and a bright orange jacket rushed toward her. He carried two rifles slung over his shoulder. A teenager trudged along several steps behind him, his expression hangdog. "Are you all right?" the man asked.

"I'm not shot," Jillian answered as she sat up in the leaves and checked her body for possible wounds.

The man pointed at Jillian and turned to look at his son. "Does she look like a deer now?"

The boy shook his head, making his overgrown blond hair flop into his eyes. "No. I'm sorry, lady. I'm glad I didn't hit you. I saw movement and I thought I saw antlers and I definitely didn't see your vest."

"I was probably blocked by the tree," she said. She didn't add, "Thank God," but she certainly thought it. The tree had taken the bullet instead of her.

The man pointed at the branches of the tree. "You must have mistaken branches for antlers. That's why we don't shoot until we can definitely tell what we're aiming at." He held out his hand

and hauled Jillian to her feet. Her knees still felt wobbly, and she wondered if a person could die from too many bursts of adrenaline in one day. Bits of sticks and leaves rained onto the ground as she beat at her clothes.

"What were you doing out in the woods anyway?" the man asked. "Don't you know it's deer season?"

Jillian gave him her best Bertie stare and pointed to her orange vest. "Of course I know. I just got turned around out here."

"Well, where you going?" the man asked. "I know these woods like the back of my hand." He looked down at his own broad hand, then thrust it out at Jillian. "I'm Rascal Johnson, and this is my boy, J.J. We're real sorry about all of this. I mean, getting your nice clothes mussed up and all."

It's better than getting my brains blown out. She forced a smile, not wanting to antagonize a man with a gun, at least not until he got her safely back to her friends. "My friends are back at this old stone foundation near the bend in the creek. It's very overgrown."

He nodded. "I know the spot. I used to play there when I was a kid. There's a root cellar in the side of the hill." He chuckled. "It made a great fort until my gran caught me using her preserves for bombs."

"When was the last time you were in it?" Jillian asked.

He thought about it for a while. "Must be nearly twenty years. I should check it out and see if any of Gran's preserves are still there. My pigs might eat them."

"That's not a good idea," Jillian said. "It's a crime scene now." She suddenly wondered if the body in the root cellar might be the man's grandmother. It would certainly keep the investigation of her death from including Bertie. "Do you know where your grandmother is?"

He gave her an odd look. "She's in the Nathan County

Retirement Home." He touched his temple. "She got too confused for us to keep up with her. Why do you want to know about my grandmother? And why is her root cellar a crime scene?"

"Because there's a dead body in it. Do you think you could help me get back there?"

"Yeah, I can, and I definitely want to see this dead body." The man stomped off into the woods, clearly expecting Jillian and his son to simply keep up with him.

Since she saw no other option, she did, falling in beside the teenager. She glanced sideways at him. He dropped his gaze when their eyes met. "Anyone can make a mistake," she said. "I'm not mad." *I'm not thrilled, but I'm not mad.*

The boy shoved his hands into the pockets of his jeans. "Thanks. I didn't want to come out here in the first place," the boy said, his voice half whisper and half mumble. "Dad loves hunting."

"Lots of folks do," Jillian said, agreeably. "Not me, but plenty of other people."

The boy nodded, his head bobbing on his long neck. She felt for him. She remembered being a teenager at odds with her own parents. It's not an easy spot. "Have you ever been out to this root cellar?"

He shook his head. "I don't walk in the woods much. I'm more into books, but Dad loves it out here." His eyes darted from side to side. "The woods are full of ticks. You can get all kinds of diseases from ticks."

"That's true." *And thanks for giving me something new to worry about.* She thought about the dive into the leaves. Were ticks burrowing into her skin even as she walked? The more she thought about it, the more her skin felt crawly.

Suddenly Rascal Johnson halted and turned to look at Jillian. "You said the root cellar was a crime scene. Which deputies are there?"

"Laura Lee Zane," Jillian said. "She called it in, but no one else had arrived before I left."

He frowned for a moment, then nodded and resumed the march through the woods without further explanation. Jillian felt sorry for the teenager. It was beginning to look like his dad might be a bit of a jerk.

When they reached the brush-choked foundation, Jillian saw that the rest of the deputies had arrived while she was gone. Deputy Gooder Jones stood chatting with Laura Lee. Not for the first time, she thought that Gooder hadn't grown up to be a bad-looking guy, except for the scowling and his sarcastic attitude. He was tall and broad-shouldered. He kept his hair short, probably to distract from a slightly receding hairline.

Gooder frowned when Jillian walked up. "I figured you had to be around here somewhere. When Laura Lee called in a skeleton found out in the boonies, I knew it had your name all over it."

Jillian was too tired to indulge in their usual war of words. She turned to thank the Johnsons for getting her back to her friends, and was surprised to see they'd left. *Hadn't Rascal said he wanted to see the dead body?* Maybe his leaving had something to do with Gooder. After all, the hunter had asked which of the deputies would be at the scene, then disappeared when they actually got there. Of course, he could have simply thought it best to avoid the deputies considering his son had nearly shot Jillian.

"Did you see the body?" Jillian asked.

"Of course. That's my job."

"I talked to Rascal Johnson in the woods. He said he's been in the root cellar before, though it's been years. Apparently it didn't come with a dead body back then."

Gooder's gaze turned to the woods behind her. "Too bad you didn't bring him with you, though I'm not surprised Rascal has been here before. This used to be part of the Johnson family land. I think they only lost it a dozen years ago or so."

"Lost it?"

"Back taxes. Everyone said his grandfather had left them pretty well-off, but apparently the money didn't last because Rascal had to sell off part of the land."

"Rascal said his grandmother kept preserves in the root cellar." Jillian gestured toward the hill.

Gooder frowned. "This is a long way from the farm for storing canned food."

"Maybe it was overflow," Laura Lee suggested. "A farm has to produce a lot of canned food."

Gooder shrugged. "I'll ask Rascal about it later. For now, why don't you tell me what y'all were doing out here."

"I already told you . . ." Laura Lee began, but Gooder held up his hand to stop the flow of words.

"I want to hear it from Jillian. It all needs to go in my report."

Jillian sighed deeply, wondering when she was going to get home. Then she launched into the story of the auction, map, break-in, and discovery. The only thing she left out was nearly getting her head blown off by a teenager.

Gooder doesn't need to know about that.

When she finally got back to Belle Haven it was well after dark. Gooder had asked her an endless stream of questions. She nearly asked him if he thought she'd somehow planted the dead body in the root cellar to annoy him. When she and Savannah were finally sent home, Jillian had ridden almost the whole way without speaking, and Savannah hadn't pushed. Jillian was dirty, cold, and starving and suspected her friend felt much the same way.

Savannah pulled in under the porte cochere. "Today sure didn't turn out the way we'd hoped."

"You got that right. Thanks for the ride."

Savannah smiled. "I'm happy I'll be going home to a quiet house."

Jillian groaned softly. She was well aware of what she would be facing. She thanked her friend again and stepped out of the car. She stopped in the laundry room and washed her hands and face in the sink. Sloughing off a little of the day's grime made her feel better—not good, but better. As she headed into the kitchen, she could see Bertie and Cornelia in the breakfast room, sipping tea.

Cornelia peered across the room and patted the chair beside her. "Come and sit. You can tell us all about the treasure."

"Didn't find any treasure," Jillian said. "I need a bath."

Cornelia's expression fell into disappointment, but Bertie simply kicked the chair out slightly. "Come and sit. You need something hot to drink, and we've got scones. I'm assuming you haven't eaten."

"Scones?" Jillian felt a tiny part of her try to perk up at the thought of food. "What kind?"

"Bacon, cheddar, and chive," Bertie said. "Now come and sit."

Jillian came and sat. She let the barrage of questions roll over her unanswered for a moment while she relished the first bite of the light, savory scone. The questions dried up as Jillian continued to chew with her eyes closed, but she could practically feel the sharp gaze of her grandmother and great-aunt. The questions wouldn't go unanswered. Jillian managed two more bites and several swallows of warm, soothing tea before she gave in. "The map led to an old stone foundation and a root cellar,"

Jillian said. "It's on the edges of the Johnson farm, apparently. Gooder said he didn't think the Johnsons owned the property anymore but apparently they used to."

"I wondered," Bertie said. "When Savannah showed us the map. I wasn't sure how far back the farm went. Do you suppose the map was old enough to be some kind of property marker? Maybe it was supposed to guide someone trying to get to the house that used to be in that spot."

"Maybe, but I doubt it." Jillian took another long sip of tea. "The root cellar had some old preserves and a very unpreserved dead body."

Cornelia gasped. "I knew it."

"You did not," Bertie snapped. "Don't go telling us some silly woo-woo stuff about it."

"You forget. I told everyone at the Sweetie Pies meeting about my dream," Cornelia said. "It certainly was *not* silly."

"You told us some vague nonsense about being certain they'd find something of significance. That could mean nearly anything."

"And this time it meant a dead body." Cornelia turned to peer at Jillian. "Did you recognize the poor man?"

Jillian shook her head. "It wasn't a man, or at least it probably wasn't. The body was little more than a skeleton but the clothes that were on it were female and Laura Lee said the person had long hair." Jillian shuddered. "I didn't look at it long enough to see that detail."

"It was a human person, dear," Cornelia said gently. "So don't call her 'it.' She won't appreciate it."

"She won't know," Bertie said. "She apparently died a long time ago if she's nothing but a skeleton. I knew that map would come to nothing good. I should never have let you both become involved with anything that used to belong to Gracie Mae Gonce."

"You like the new furniture," Cornelia reminded her.

"Not that much."

Jillian took another sip of tea and held up her hand. "Bertie, Savannah told me that you were in some kind of feud with Gracie Mae Gonce. What was that all about?"

"I was never in a feud with anyone," Bertie snapped. "And I'm not going to talk about Gracie Mae Gonce. I'm annoyed that she's still able to make me miserable." With that she stood. "Good night. I have to be up early for work."

Jillian had to as well, but she wasn't going to head up until she had some answers. Bertie's behavior had only made her curious. A curiosity so strong it even held her exhaustion at bay. She reached out and put her hand on Cornelia's arm. "Tell me about this feud."

"It really was a long time ago," Cornelia said.

"And yet it's still making Bertie tense, so tell me."

Cornelia fussed around straightening up the table. "We both knew Gracie Mae when we were children. She was a crazy competitive little thing, as I remember. She always had to run the fastest in races or get the best grades. And, my, how that child would crow when she won. It was harmless, but so annoying."

"Considering how competitive Bertie can be, I can see how the two of them would clash," Jillian said.

Cornelia sighed as she carefully stacked the used plates. "Most of the other children didn't really care. We were happy to let Gracie Mae win if it made her so happy. But not Bertie. She hated all the bragging so she began to truly compete. And your grandmother was every bit as bright and good at everything. The two of them were fairly evenly matched. Sometimes Gracie Mae would win, sometimes Bertie."

"Sounds normal enough."

"It was, right up until they both were sweet on the same boy, Jack Harper. That boy was a charmer with hair as red as a flame and a grin to set a girl's heart fluttering. Bertie wasn't one to fling herself at a boy, but you could tell she liked him. That's when Gracie Mae really got crazy."

"Grandpa Jack must have loved having two girls after him," Jillian said, laughing at the idea of her sweet, quiet grandfather being so popular with the ladies.

"He actually didn't know Bertie was sweet on him, but he sure couldn't miss Gracie Mae's interest. I think he was embarrassed, if you want to know the truth. He did his best to avoid Gracie Mae. Then Jack fell in love with Bertie, and Gracie Mae seemed to focus on beating Bertie at everything else. If Bertie entered baked goods at the county fair, Gracie Mae had to send the same item. Sometimes Bertie won, sometimes Gracie Mae. But if Gracie Mae lost, you can be sure she'd find something else, someplace else, to compete with Bertie."

"How come I didn't know about any of this?" Jillian asked as she gently swirled the last of her tea around in her mug. "Did it end before I was born?"

"Hardly. Gracie Mae met and married Wallace Gonce. He was a nice, dull guy. His only interesting feature was his ginger-colored hair. I always thought he resembled a slightly faded version of Jack, though Bertie said she could never see it. I think she might have said that just to be difficult since it was plain as day. The two looked like brothers."

"Gracie Mae married someone because he looked like Grandpa? That's just strange."

"I never asked her about it, but I suspect so." Cornelia sighed. "I hoped it was over then. Gracie Mae finally had her version of Jack, and I figured married life would keep her busy. Bertie had your mama, and Gracie Mae gave birth to a son. She named him Jack. I can't believe her husband let her do that. At any rate, she acted like having that boy was some kind of win over Bertie, since Bertie had a girl. It wasn't right at all."

"That is the strangest thing I ever heard," Jillian said. "What did Bertie think of all this?"

"Bertie didn't talk about it much. When she did, she told me Gracie Mae was only embarrassing herself. That was about the time I met Raymond and got married. Raymond and I moved away so I didn't think much about Gracie Mae. I figured it was just so much foolishness and so did Bertie."

"But the feud wasn't over."

"It was never a feud exactly. Just one woman jealous to death of another. It did get quiet until your mama was a teenager. Seems she was sweet on Jack Gonce for a while, until Bertie put her foot down. There was too much crazy in that boy's blood for Bertie's daughter."

Jillian harrumphed. "I can't imagine that moved my mother much."

Cornelia laughed. "Not so much. What did put an end to the whole thing was the moment your mama met your daddy. It was love at first sight for those two. They were both nomads, free spirits, or whatever you call folks who follow every silly thing that comes into their heads. All I heard after that from Bertie was complaints about your mama."

Jillian swallowed the last tepid sip of tea. "I can imagine."

"After I'd been married for a while, I got to missing all the Moss Hollow gossip. That's how it is when you're married. At first, you're not a bit interested in anything but each other, but slowly the world creeps back in. I started going to the Sweetie Pies meetings. That's how I found out Gracie Mae—bless her heart—still loved doing things solely to get Bertie's goat. She was still good at it too."

"So it sounds. Still, since this was a lifelong problem, I can't believe I didn't know."

Cornelia stood and picked up the dirty dishes. "Your mama never talked about it all because it was a sore spot for your daddy.

And Bertie never talked about it either. She found the whole thing undignified. She was just glad when the Gonces moved away."

"But Savannah said Gracie Mae never gave up fanning the feud," Jillian said as she stood and picked up the plate of scones and followed Cornelia to the kitchen area. "Something to do with her restaurant."

Cornelia set the plates in the sink. "I had hoped, for a while, that I'd be able to reconcile Bertie and Gracie Mae. I couldn't see any point to the feud, and I was hoping they'd give it up. Of course, I was married then and everything in life seemed possible. I even invited Gracie Mae to join the Sweetie Pies."

Jillian gasped, knowing that couldn't have gone well. "Did Bertie know that was you?"

"No. She wasn't as good at reading my guilty face when I didn't live with her. I'd rather you didn't tell her. As you probably know, Gracie Mae wasn't interested in reconciling. Not long after that, the Gonces up and closed the restaurant and left town. It was a relief, to be honest."

"Savannah said as much," Jillian said as she slipped the remainder of the scones from the plate into a plastic container. "She said the Sweetie Pies might have broken up if the Gonces hadn't left. No one wanted to come to the meetings anymore."

"Yes, that was a bad miscalculation on my part. It's an idea that came from Raymond. He knew I was fretting about the feud, but I should have known better than to follow Raymond's advice when it came to Gracie Mae and Bertie. He was terrible at dealing with drama." Cornelia popped the last of the dirty dishes into the dishwasher. "It's getting late, and I'm going to bed. She opened the fridge and took out a cold slice of bacon. "I saved one. Raymond always did love bacon."

Jillian shook her head in amusement as her aunt left the room with Possum's treat in one hand. At least the cat was going to have a good night. She snapped the lid on the container of scones and carried a damp cloth over to wipe the breakfast table.

The things her aunt had told her were interesting, but they did nothing to explain why there was a blood-stained map in the Gonce's storage unit, a map that had led them to a dead body. Jillian shuddered at the memory of the skeleton on the hard-packed dirt floor. If the body turned out to be Gracie Mae Gonce, the woman's obsessive feud would bring trouble right to the front steps of Belle Haven. Again.

Autumn continued to drive customers to the bakery for pies and pastries and pumpkin spice *everything*, but Jillian found that even the bustle of work couldn't completely take her mind off the horrific discovery in the root cellar. The distressing truth was that she'd seen dead bodies before, but the sight of a woman left behind, seemly forgotten, haunted Jillian's dreams and made her jumpy during the day. She couldn't shake the fear that another shoe would drop soon, and it would drop on her or someone she loved.

The painful suspense lasted for days with no word as to the identity of the woman they'd found. Friday found Jillian in the breakfast room, sipping coffee and pondering whether she had room for one more fluffy biscuit. Aunt Cornelia caught her gazing at the breadbasket and passed it over. Jillian held up a hand. "No, I think I'm better off admiring them from afar."

A knock at the side door gained their attention. "Are we expecting anyone?"

"At this time of morning?" Cornelia said. "It's still dark, dear."

Jillian walked through the utility rooms and opened the door that led to the porte cochere. Deputy Gooder Jones stood in the doorway, scowling. He shifted his belt, a maneuver that reminded Jillian of Barney Fife from *The Andy Griffith Show*, a comparison that wouldn't improve Gooder's feelings about her, so she wisely chose not to share it with him. "I need to talk to y'all," he said.

"You'll need to specify," Jillian said, blocking his way into the house mostly for the fun of being annoying. "With which of the Belle Haven residents do you wish to speak?"

He growled through gritted teeth. "All of them."

Jillian stepped back, and Gooder passed her. That's when she saw Laura Lee still under the porte cochere, looking embarrassed. "Hi, Jillian."

"Hi, Laura Lee," she said. "Am I going to enjoy this visit?"

Laura Lee sighed and answered quietly. "I seriously doubt it, though you've already annoyed Gooder. That's got to be fun."

"It has its moments."

They walked together into the kitchen and found Gooder had already barreled into the breakfast nook. Bertie and Cornelia were looking at up at him with no sign of alarm.

"Would you care for a biscuit, Gooder?" Cornelia asked, holding up the basket. "I made them this morning."

Cornelia's biscuits were famous throughout Moss Hollow, and Jillian saw a flicker of weakness pass over Gooder's face, but he shook his head. "No, thank you. I'm here to let you know we've identified the body in the root cellar. It's definitely Gracie Mae Gonce."

Cornelia gasped softly, her pleasant smile slipping away to sadness. "The poor thing. Have you contacted Wallace?"

"We're looking for him," Gooder admitted, then turned to Bertie. "But right now I need to ask you about your relationship with Mrs. Gonce."

"I've known her since we were children," Bertie said. "She was frustrating, but it's still sad."

"Those aren't the words I've heard used to describe your relationship," Gooder said. "Sheriff Henderson says y'all got along about like oil and water."

"If Coy Henderson has things to say to me about Gracie Mae, he ought to come along and say them," Bertie said tartly. "The woman spent years trying to get my goat. With as much effort as she put in, sometimes she had to score a hit or two, but I had no desire to hurt her."

"Still, you must have been relieved when she left town."

Cornelia broke in. "Everyone was relieved. Gracie Mae was an uncomfortable person to know. I tried to befriend the poor thing, but she was impossible."

"Why are you bothering my grandmother?" Jillian demanded. "Because Gracie Mae beat her out of a couple county fair baking competitions? That's ridiculous. I thought husbands were prime suspects in murder cases. Why isn't the investigation focusing on Wallace Gonce? Especially considering he apparently didn't file a missing person's report before he left Moss Hollow."

"We definitely want to speak to the husband," Laura Lee interjected, getting the stink eye from Gooder.

"Assuming he's still alive," Gooder said. "We can't find him, and his wife is certainly dead. The last known address for him is a dead end. For all we know, the husband is dead as well. Seems like the operative word across the board is 'dead.'"

Jillian huffed. "So now you're imagining a murderer who scatters bodies all over the Moss Hollow area like some kind of creepy Johnny Appleseed? That's ridiculous. The man undoubtedly killed his wife and fled town. So why are you bothering my grandmother?"

"We are looking for Wallace Gonce and his son, Jack, but until we find them, I intend to follow all other possible leads."

Bertie stood and folded her arms over her chest. "And other than some silly feud, which was mostly in Gracie Mae's head, what other leads do you have?"

"I'm not in the habit of discussing details of my cases with persons of interest," he said.

Behind him, Laura Lee mouthed, "None."

Gooder opened his notebook and flipped through pages. He read off the date the Gonce's country restaurant closed. "Do you know what you were doing that day?"

"What day of the week was it?" Bertie asked.

Gooder looked uncomfortable for a moment, shifting his weight from one foot to the other. Behind him, Jillian saw Laura Lee pull out her phone and began swiping screens.

"What difference does that make?" he snapped.

"It will help me answer your question."

"It was a Friday," Laura Lee answered, looking up from her phone.

"Then I was putting away new stock," Bertie said. "That's the middle of the month and a Friday, so it's a fairly sure thing that I got a delivery that day. So I was updating inventory and trying to find a place in my storage room for sacks of flour and sugar."

"Is there anyone who can confirm that?"

"Lenora probably, though I'm only guessing on that being a delivery date, I'd have to check my records. The day doesn't stand out to me. I didn't find out about the restaurant closing for a couple of days after it happened since I don't have to drive that way to go to and from Belle Haven. I do remember how I learned about the restaurant closing. A couple of customers at the bakery mentioned it." Bertie took a step closer to him. "Now if that's enough, I need to get to work. Some of us know what our job entails, and we do it."

Gooder's face reddened at that. "That's it for now. But once we find out how Gracie Mae died, I'll be back."

"You don't even know how she died?" Jillian said. "So you don't even know that anyone killed her. You're just here annoying us for no real reason."

"Until I know for sure, I have to treat it as a suspicious death," Gooder said. "And it doesn't seem reasonable that Gracie Mae Gonce would hike out in the woods to property that didn't even belong to her in order to drop dead of natural causes."

His remark reminded Jillian of something. "Have you talked to the Johnsons about the body? Since it was their property."

"It's on my to-do list," Gooder admitted.

"Then maybe you best go get it done," Bertie said, making shooing motions with her hands. "Now let me get to work, or I'm going to call your grandmother and tell her what a nuisance you're being."

Gooder winced at that. His grandmother was well-known for being feisty and quick to poke wayward grandchildren with her bony fingers.

Jillian hated to send him off with so much of his attention still on Bertie. "Have you looked into the guy who bid against Cornelia at the storage unit auction?" she asked. "He seemed awfully eager to have that unit. The same unit where we found the map that led us to a dead body. Plus, I'm fairly certain that he's the one who tried to break into our house *and* I saw him in the woods after I found the body."

Gooder's eyes narrowed. "Why is this the first I've heard about him being in the woods?"

"I forgot," Jillian admitted. "Hey, I got lost and with the dead body . . . I just forgot." *Plus, someone almost shot me*, she added mentally.

Gooder shrugged. "Fine. I'll put him on the list of people I want to talk with as soon as I find out who he is. What did he look like?"

Jillian slipped her phone out of the front pocket of her white pants, a color she normally wouldn't choose in the fall, but it was the traditional baker's choice because it hid flour. She woke up the phone and pulled up the photo she'd taken of the man. "Here he is."

Gooder barked out a laugh. "Could you have taken a worse photo? I can barely see any of his face at all. This guy could be anyone. He could be my dad, except he's got too much hair."

"He ducked as soon as he saw me taking the photo and with good reason since he came back later to try to break into Belle Haven."

He pointed at Jillian. "Don't remind me. You should have sense enough to know to call us for a break-in."

"He didn't get all the way in," Jillian said. "Possum took care of him. Plus, he was wearing a ski mask."

"Then what makes you think it's this guy?" Gooder pointed at the photo on the phone.

"Because when I saw him again in the woods near the root cellar his face was all scratched up. I'm pretty sure I told you all this. Chasing him is how I got lost in the first place. Possum gave him the scratches."

"Maybe," Gooder conceded. "Or maybe your vivid imagination ran away with you and you saw a totally different person who had scratched his face on the briars that are everywhere around there." He jacked up his shirt sleeve to show off a ragged scratch. "One of them got me too."

Bertie stepped around Jillian to crowd Gooder, looking up at him. Bertie was short and Gooder was tall, but the tiny woman still clearly intimidated him. "It still seems to me that part of doing your job would be looking for this man."

"And it will," he said. "But don't think this is going away. Once you check your records for your whereabouts on the day the Gonce's restaurant closed, I'd appreciate a call."

"You'll get one," Bertie agreed.

Gooder left with Laura Lee in tow, though she flashed a quick smile at Jillian as they walked out. Jillian stood at the side door and watched them climb into the sheriff's department vehicle. She'd wanted to believe Gooder wouldn't up and arrest Bertie. He'd generally been a better cop than that, but she'd still feel better if she gave him something tangible to look at instead, such as the whereabouts of Wallace Gonce.

Walking back into the kitchen where Bertie and Cornelia were cleaning up from breakfast, Jillian joined in. They cleaned up quietly for a few minutes, each caught up in their own thoughts, though Jillian figured that they were all about the same subject.

Finally Cornelia folded the kitchen towel neatly and hung it up on the bar over the sink. "I'm going to try using the tear-out cards," she said. "They may reveal what is really going on here."

Jillian groaned. Having not heard anything about them for a while, she'd hoped her aunt had given up on trying to contact the spirit realm using subscription cards torn from the magazines at the beauty parlor. She tried to console herself with the idea that it could be worse. Cornelia could find out about real tarot cards.

"You're being ridiculous," Bertie told her. "I don't know where you get these ideas."

Cornelia raised her head high. "Call me names if you want, but at least I'm trying to help." Then Cornelia sailed out of the kitchen with her chin so high Jillian was surprised she didn't run into something.

"Do you mind if I come in to work a little late?" Jillian asked her grandmother. "I want to drive out to the storage unit company and talk to the owner, Robert Skiff. He may recognize this photo of the other bidder, even though Gooder didn't."

"Let me see it," Bertie said. She took the camera and studied the photo. "This really is a horrible photo. How could anyone recognize someone from this?"

"His clothes show up fairly well," Jillian said. "So if Robert Skiff knows him that might be enough. Plus, someone must have been paying for the storage unit for years. I'm assuming that someone was Wallace Gonce. So I may be able to get an address to pass on to Gooder."

"You don't have to get involved in this," Bertie said. "I'm not worried about Gooder Jones."

Jillian nodded. "But I'll feel better if he has somewhere else to focus his investigation. Remember what happened when all of Moss Hollow thought I might be a murderer? It killed business."

"That's because they thought you had poisoned Nadine Belmont," Bertie said, "using a bakery cupcake as the murder weapon. This is totally different."

"Unless it turns out Gracie Mae was poisoned," Jillian said.

Bertie frowned darkly. "Fine. You go do whatever you must. But don't make a day of it. We've got plenty of orders to fill."

"I won't dawdle. I only want to look the man in the face when I show him this photo. That way I'll know if he lies to me."

"Why would he lie?"

Jillian shrugged. "Why would anyone?"

Her grandmother peered at her. "You know, you're growing very cynical. I blame all those years in California."

"Right," Jillian said. "It couldn't be the things we've had to deal with since I got home. As you pointed out, this isn't the first time someone at Belle Haven has been suspected of a crime. It's a wonder Gooder doesn't check here every time there's a crime in Nathan County. Frankly, it's getting a little old."

"Just be careful," Bertie said. "Trouble seems to be attracted to you like flies on horse biscuits."

Jillian winced. "Ew. Couldn't you have chosen bees to honey?"

Bertie smiled. "I call it as I see it. Now get on with your errands. The sooner you get to work, the better."

Jillian managed to arrive at the storage unit company as Robert Skiff was opening up for the morning. She waited while he put on a pot of coffee, then showed him the photo on her phone.

Robert scratched his head while he peered at the blurry photo. "He doesn't look familiar." He handed back the phone. "I'm sorry. I've only lived in Moss Hollow about three years, and I spend most of my time here. I haven't met that many people other than the ones who've rented storage units. Plus, that's a really terrible photo."

"Three years. So you didn't live anywhere around here when that storage unit was rented?"

He shook his head. "I was still in New Jersey then. A lot of these units were already rented when I bought the place. You know, you're not the only one asking questions about that unit."

Jillian nodded. "I figured the police would have been by."

"Yeah, they were," he agreed as he glanced at the filling coffee pot and fetched a couple mugs from a shelf over the coffee maker. He handed her one. "But I also got a call from a man who wouldn't leave his name. He demanded to know if anyone had found a map in the unit." He lifted one broad shoulder. "I told him I only rent the things. I don't tour them."

"How did he react to that?" Jillian asked, running her thumb idly over a chip in the rim of the mug.

"He was pretty steamed, but there was nothing I could tell him."

"When did the police come by?"

"Well, Saturday night, of course," he said, his eyes turning toward the pot again. Coffee still trickled into it. "But again yesterday."

"Saturday night?"

He rubbed his slightly stubbly chin. "Yeah, after the break-in."

"Break-in!"

"The deputy thought it was kids," he said, turning back to the pot and filling his mug. "Someone broke into the office and pulled all the files onto the floor. It took me days to get everything back in the right folder. Nothing was stolen, far as I could tell."

"How would you have been able to tell if someone took

something from one of the older folders?" she asked. "You said most of them predate your ownership."

"I've been through them all. I have to. I have bills to send out and all." He stirred several packets of sugar into the coal-colored coffee. "You going to have some coffee?"

She found the color of the coffee a little alarming, but didn't want to offend the man while he was being so talkative, so she held out her mug so he could fill it. "Do you have an address or any other contact information for whoever rented the storage unit that my aunt bought at the auction?"

"The owner of record is Wallace Gonce," he said, pausing to take a sip of his coffee, then winced and added another packet of sugar and some artificial creamer. "But the last few bills I sent to that address came back and the phone number has been disconnected. That's why the unit ended up going to auction."

Jillian nodded. "What city did you send the bills to?"

"Macon." He looked up at the clock on the wall and gently took the untouched mug of coffee from Jillian. "If you don't mind, my favorite show is about to come on. I hate to miss it. It's all about finding treasure in junk. I figure it's research so I can judge the value in the junk people leave behind here."

Jillian almost warned him about treasure hunting and how it can lead to dead bodies, but she decided not to rain on his parade. He'd been as helpful as he could be. Before she left, she had one last question. "In the files that were trashed, would there have been any information about who won the Saturday auctions?"

"Of course." He grinned proudly. "I keep meticulous records."

Jillian thanked him and headed out the door. She'd probably just discovered how the mysterious bidder had found Cornelia's address. And if that man also made the mysterious phone call about the map, he definitely had some answers that Jillian wanted to hear. Now all she had to do was find him.

Jillian zipped up the front of her jacket as she walked from the tourist parking lot near the old train depot that now housed the historical society. For some reason, the town had decided it was the perfect time to work on the two side streets that allowed access to the lot behind the bakery. That made both parking behind the bakery and deliveries a nuisance, though Jillian didn't really mind the extra walking time. The day was cool, though far from cold, and the streets were busy with shoppers.

The tiny bell over the door tinkled as she stepped into the customer area of the bakery. She saw customers seated at most of the tables, chatting and sipping some of the bakery's fresh, rich coffee. The line at the counter was short, and Jillian definitely recognized the man at the head of it.

She slipped around the end of the counter and grabbed an apron from the shelf as she walked up to the register, standing beside Maggie, who worked the front counter. "Hi, Hunter."

The smile he turned on her was as warm as a Georgia morning in June. "Jillian! I was afraid I was going to miss you. I'm picking up more cookies. Our clients are very particular about their cookies."

Jillian nodded. "Folks in Moss Hollow tend to resist change."

"So I've noticed." He collected his change from Maggie, then gestured toward the seating area. "Do you have a minute?"

"Of course." Jillian knew Hunter was about the only person her grandmother would never grumble about keeping Jillian away from work. She walked back around the counter and followed Hunter to the empty table near the restroom. She considered teasing him about picking the best seat in the house, but the serious expression on his face dissuaded her. "What's up?"

"I wanted to find out if you're all right," he said, looking at her face intently. "I know finding that skeleton must have been upsetting."

Jillian had seen far too many dead bodies since coming back to Moss Hollow, but she appreciated his concern. "It certainly wasn't the treasure we'd hoped for. Have you seen it?" Hunter was also the country coroner, so Jillian assumed the bones had ended up at the funeral home.

"I have," he said. "Though I believe the remains will be released as soon as they find the woman's husband or son."

Jillian's eyes widened. "So you're sure it's Gracie Mae?"

He nodded.

"Did you test the blood sample from the map? Was it from Gracie Mae?"

"It wasn't human," he said. "I could narrow it down a little more on type of animal, but I'm not set up for extensive testing. Whatever bled on that hide, it wasn't Gracie Mae. And I suspect the bloodstain was much older. It's probably not related."

"And you're sure the remains were hers?"

"I'm sure. I actually found the clue that helped identify the body. Though the body was mostly bones, as you know, I could tell it was an older woman who had suffered two broken legs at some point, both of which had been set with pins. That's what identified her. It wasn't hard to get copies of Gracie Mae's x-rays from the car accident."

"I remember that accident." Jillian and Hunter looked up to see Bertie walking over. "The crash happened about twenty years ago." She looked directly at Jillian. "About the time you left Moss Hollow."

Jillian frowned. "I'm surprised I never heard about it. It must have been a bad accident to break both her legs."

Bertie nodded. "It was pretty rough. From what I heard Gracie Mae ran off the road to avoid hitting a deer. She hit a tree instead. It totaled the car and nearly totaled her. She was in the hospital for quite a while."

"I saw the breaks," Hunter said. "I imagine she must have been pinned in the car to do that kind of damage."

"I believe they had to cut her out of the car," Bertie said. "I tried to make a friendly visit to the hospital after it happened. I'd hoped to settle things between us with flowers, but she actually threatened to call security on me."

Jillian could tell Bertie was still deeply offended by the memory. "I never heard about any of this," she said.

Bertie waved a hand. "It wasn't important. And I suppose it all turned out well for Gracie Mae. Right after she got out of the hospital, she bought that restaurant and outfitted it with a kitchen I would have loved to have. All new everything."

Jillian whistled. "That must have cost a lot."

"Apparently Gracie Mae had amazing insurance because Wallace sure didn't make enough money up at the power company to pay for all that."

"That doesn't make sense," Hunter said. "Any insurance payments would be needed for the medical bills and car repairs or replacement."

"Maybe they didn't get a new car and opened a restaurant instead," Jillian suggested. "If Gracie Mae's car was fancy, that could have been a good payday."

"Gracie Mae's car was held together by baling wire and bubble gum," Bertie said. "And the car they bought to replace it wasn't much better. But I always assumed they got some kind of money for emotional suffering or some such. I could picture Gracie Mae milking the system somehow."

Hunter's expression reflected the same doubt Jillian felt. "I really don't see how."

Jillian had to agree. After all, the insurance company could hardly have sued the deer. The whole story sounded dubious, but it left a big question. How did Gracie Mae get the money for the restaurant? "Maybe she took out some big loans."

"If so, I suppose Annalise's husband could find out," Bertie said. Annalise Reed was a member of the Southern Sweetie Pies, and her husband, Byron, was vice president at the bank. "If anyone in Moss Hollow takes out a loan, his bank is where they'd get the money. We're not exactly crowded with banks or lenders."

"A loan that size would be difficult to get," Hunter said. "Especially if they didn't have much collateral or income. Maybe they had someone co-sign for it."

"It's too bad Byron would never tell us," Jillian said.

Bertie looked deep in thought. "Yeah, too bad." She excused herself and walked back toward the kitchen. Jillian had the feeling Bertie might be the best person to come up with the information about the bank loan. Her grandmother was hard to resist when she wanted something. Jillian felt a mild pang of sympathy for Byron. If he and Annalise were back from their trip, his life was about to get complicated.

"Have I mentioned how glad I am that your grandmother is usually on my side?" Hunter asked, his eyes sparkling with amusement over the edge of his coffee cup.

"She is a force of nature," Jillian agreed. "But I do think I'm going to see what I can learn about that traffic accident."

"I don't suppose it would do any good if I asked you to be careful," Hunter said.

Jillian made a face at him. "I'm always careful, thank you very much."

"Sure you are." He rose from his chair. "I have to get back to work. If you do find out anything, I'd appreciate it if you keep me in the loop."

Jillian held up her hand. "Can I ask one last question?"

"Of course."

"How did Gracie Mae die?"

Hunter's face turned serious. "As coroner, I really couldn't tell you the cause of death. It's up to the sheriff's department to release that kind of information. But since I couldn't determine what killed her, I have no information to release."

"You couldn't tell what killed her?" Jillian's eyes widened. "So it could have been natural causes?"

"The body was down to bones. It could have been a lot of things that I would not find evidence of in the bones." He sighed. "Again, I have to run. Take care, okay? I worry about you. Sometimes you can be a force of nature yourself, Miss Green."

Jillian stood and pushed in her chair. "I'll take that as a compliment, Mr. Greyson."

He smiled warmly. "You should take anything I say about you as a compliment, as it is most certainly meant as one."

Jillian felt her cheeks warm at his admiring look, and she ducked her head, hoping to hide the blush. "Well, you have a good day."

He nodded, then wove through the tables and slipped out the door, leaving the light tinkle of the bell in his wake. Jillian glanced toward the kitchen, knowing she should head in and get to work, but she wanted to start the ball rolling on learning about Gracie Mae's accident, so she quickly called Laura Lee Zane.

After Jillian explained what she wanted to the young deputy, Laura Lee whistled softly. "Gooder Jones will throw a tantrum and a half if he hears of me helping you." Then she chuckled. "So, of course, I will. I'll call back as soon as I know anything."

"I appreciate it," Jillian said. "But don't do anything that will get you in trouble."

"What fun is life without trouble?" Laura Lee asked.

As soon as they ended the call, Bertie tapped on the display case to get Jillian's attention. "You planning to do any work today at all? In case you haven't noticed, we're right busy here."

"Coming," Jillian said as she dashed around the counter and headed into the bakery kitchen. *Time to whip pumpkin!*

Jillian had mixed up a half dozen loaves of pumpkin tea bread and moved on to making pumpkin spice cookies when her phone rang. She backed away from the mixer and pulled her phone from the bib pocket of her apron. As soon as she saw the caller was Laura Lee, she quickly answered the call. "What did you find out?"

"Well, hello to you too, Jillian," Laura Lee said with a laugh. "How's your morning going? Mine has been busy."

"Sorry," Jillian said. "I'm a little on edge I guess. Now will you tell me what you learned?"

"Since you asked nicely, yes. This is going to surprise you. Gracie Mae's car accident took place on a stretch of road we were all driving very recently. The accident occurred right by the Johnson farm."

"That's an interesting coincidence."

"Isn't it?" Laura Lee said. "The rest of the report is a little confusing. Gracie Mae Gonce told investigators that she ran off the road in an attempt to avoid a deer, but there is clear evidence in these accident report photos that she was not the only car on the road. I'm seeing skid marks going in two different directions."

"Did anyone identify the second car?" Jillian asked.

"I can't see any suggestion they even tried," Laura Lee said. "Gracie Mae's story was consistent every time she told it, and so it became the official record. But *I* certainly find that second set of tracks interesting."

"Can you tell anything about them from the photos?"

"I'm no forensics expert, but if I had to guess, I'd say they were pick-up tracks. The wheelbase is definitely broader than the one on Gracie Mae's car tracks. The car accident isn't an open investigation, but I may be able to get someone to look at these photos in light of Gracie Mae's highly suspicious death."

"There's a lot of years between the two events," Jillian said, playing devil's advocate, even though she strongly felt the two events were connected.

"That's why I said 'may' instead of 'will,' but I promise to do my best. I'll let you know if anything turns up."

"Thanks," Jillian said, tapping the phone against her chin. She was pulled from her reverie when Bertie clanged against the thick metal mixing bowl with a spoon.

"Who left cookie dough half done?" Bertie demanded.

"Me," Jillian yelped. "I'm coming right back to it."

Her grandmother shook her head. "What am I going to do with you?"

Nag me forever? Jillian hurriedly checked over the recipe to see that she'd put all the ingredients in the bowl. She didn't want to miss something, especially with all the missing links she was already dealing with. As she finally flipped on the mixer, she wished the details of Gracie Mae's death would come together as easily.

When Jillian pulled the last sheet of softly puffed pumpkin cookies from the oven, the scent of spice in the air was heady. She pushed the tray into the cooling rack and rolled the rack away from the oven. Bertie caught the other end of the rack and hauled it toward the decorating station where it would be out of the way since they didn't have any cakes to do. Once the cookies cooled enough to remove from the tray, Lenora would dip the tops in a bowl of icing to give them a sweet finish.

"I'm done with my to-do list," Jillian said to her grandmother. "I'd like to take a late lunch.

Bertie raised an eyebrow. "Is this going to be one of those lunches that stretch until dinner?"

Jillian mimed drawing an X on her chest. "Nope, I'll be back soon as I can. Cross my heart."

"You're going to keep poking at this thing with Gracie Mae, aren't you?"

"Yes. It came to us first, and I want to do something about it before it becomes a serious problem. Belle Haven was broken into."

"No one had to break anything, you hadn't locked the doors yet."

"That is not the point," Jillian insisted. "I don't want this turning into another big mess with one of us under serious suspicion of murder. I can tell you right now that it's not a pleasant place to be."

"Fine. Go do what you must, but get back here as quick as you can. This is still a working bakery, and we have plenty to do."

Jillian didn't give Bertie time to change her mind. She was across the kitchen in seconds, pulling off her ugly pink hairnet and the long white apron, now streaked with flour and cinnamon. Out in the front of the bakery, she made a beeline for the coatrack where she'd left her jacket, but someone stepped into her path before she could reach it. Jillian jerked to a stop as Wanda Jean wagged a finger at her. "You promised to let us know immediately how the treasure hunt went, but Maudie and I had to learn about it from Jasmine over at the Clip & Curl."

"It was totally embarrassing," Maudie called from a nearby table. "Not knowing the scoop about something involving so many Sweetie Pies."

"I'm so sorry," Jillian said. "But I'm sure you're all up to date now. I'm afraid I have to run."

Wanda Jean narrowed her eyes suspiciously. "You're going off to poke around somewhere, aren't you?"

Jillian ducked around her and grabbed her coat. "I'm going to run an errand. I'll see you on Sunday and catch everyone up. Have a nice day." She spun and practically ran for the bakery door.

As it was a truly beautiful day in late autumn, the afternoon sun slanting through the windshield warmed the car so much that Jillian had to crack the windows. There was still plenty of green all around her as autumn in Georgia lacked the dramatic flair that she knew was true farther north. Still, she loved the way it lightened the air and made being outside so pleasant. It was such an enjoyable drive, Jillian was almost sad when she rounded a bend in the road and the Johnson farm came into view.

She pulled up in the driveway and spotted someone squatting next to a big green tractor, his back to her. "Excuse me?"

The man at the tractor twisted around, holding a forearm up to shade his eyes. He smiled slightly and Jillian recognized him. It was Rascal Johnson. "I remember you. You're not lost again, are you?"

"No, I'm here on purpose. I imagine you heard whose bones we found in your granny's root cellar."

His smile slipped away and he nodded. "I'm right sorry for her family."

Jillian shoved her hands in her jacket pockets. "You don't happen to know where Wallace Gonce lives now?"

The farmer looked surprised. "Nope. I barely knew the man. I knew Gracie Mae a mite better than Wallace, and I didn't really know her much."

"I imagine having her crash into a tree outside your yard was a rough way to meet someone."

He stood up, pulled out a rag from his pocket and began wiping his hands. "I didn't actually meet Gracie Mae Gonce until she opened that restaurant of hers. They surely did have good food."

Jillian opened her eyes wide. "Someone crashed into a tree in front of your house and you didn't go out to see?"

He laughed dryly. "Don't get me wrong. I would have hustled out to help, for sure. I wasn't home. I'd gone to Atlanta to visit an old friend. I didn't get home until the day after the accident. My wife told me about it, of course."

"Your wife saw the wreck?" Jillian asked.

He shook his head. "No, only the aftermath. She made the phone call to get help. They had to pry that woman out of the car. She'd smacked good and proper into that big oak across the road." He waved vaguely in the direction of the road.

"Do you think I could talk to your wife?" Jillian asked. "She might remember some details of the wreck."

He shook his head. "I wish you could. My wife died of cancer two years ago."

"Oh, I'm so sorry."

"Me too," he said. "Every single day." He shoved the rag back into his pocket. "What sends you out here to ask questions anyway? You writing a book?"

Jillian chuckled weakly at his attempt at a joke. "No. I found the body and I guess it's left me wanting to know more about Gracie Mae when she was alive. You know, to put her in my head as a person and not only a pile of bones and rags."

"I can understand that." He glanced back toward the tractor. "I didn't know her much, though. Just at the restaurant, like I said. You can probably find other folks in town who knew her better." He gave another look toward the tractor.

Jillian took the hint. "I'll do that. Thank you for talking to me."

"No problem. You be careful if you go walking in anymore woods."

"I do believe I'm done with that for a while."

"Good thinking." He turned back to his tractor and Jillian walked to her car, discouraged that her visit hadn't turned up anything useful. She made the drive back to the bakery with less enthusiasm, her appreciation for the scenery and the day now colored by her disappointment.

She parked in the tourist lot again and headed toward the bakery. As she passed the old Cooper's Pharmacy Building, turned years ago into the public library, a staccato tapping caught her attention. She turned to face the big window that gave passersby a view into one of the larger lounge areas in the library. Josi Rosenschein waved her in.

"Hi Josi," Jillian whispered as she walked through the heavy front doors.

"I wanted to make sure you were okay," Josi said, then she wrinkled her nose. "I heard about your discovery on your treasure hunt. That couldn't have been pleasant."

"No, it truly wasn't. And while poor Gracie Mae may not have been my first dead body, it may have been the saddest. To think of someone being left for years in that old root cellar." Jillian shook her head. "There's something horribly lonely about that."

"No doubt. I didn't know her, of course, but I've heard from several patrons that she had a wonderful restaurant." Josi was a recent addition to Moss Hollow. It was hard for Jillian to believe she'd known Josi for such a short time. The quiet librarian's loyalty and kindness had already made her a good friend.

"Is that all you've heard about her?" Jillian asked.

Again Josi made a face. "I heard she and Bertie didn't get along very well."

"Apparently that's an understatement." Jillian sighed. "I can't believe I didn't know anything about that. I must have been the most oblivious teenager in the world."

Josi laughed. "I think that might be considered redundant. It's not abnormal to be a little self-absorbed when you're a teenager."

"You know, I wonder if you could possibly help me find Gracie Mae's family. I know you're an impressive researcher."

"Flattery isn't necessary. I'll give it a try. Her husband's name was Wallace, right?"

"Yes, and her son is Jack. Anything you could find out would be super."

"I'll do what I can and let you know."

Jillian gave her friend an impulsive hug. "Thanks so much. I have to run back to the bakery. I promised Bertie I wouldn't dawdle."

"Tell her it's my fault."

"That wouldn't be a very nice way to repay you for doing me a favor," Jillian said. "I'll see you later."

When Jillian walked into the customer area, she was glad to see Maudie and Wanda Jean had left, so she'd be spared another distraction. As she slipped behind the counter, she whispered to Maggie. "How's the climate in the kitchen?"

"You should be fine," Maggie whispered back. "Bertie hasn't started ranting yet."

"Excellent." Jillian snatched a fresh hairnet from the box and headed into the kitchen, twisting her hair up under the net as she walked. She spotted Lenora Ryan at the decorating table, a smear of vanilla icing bright against her brown cheek. "I thought we didn't have any cake orders."

"One came in," the tall woman said. Lenora had been working at the bakery for as long as Jillian could remember. If Bertie had a good right hand, it was Lenora. "Mrs. Miller over at the elementary school wants two dozen cupcakes with turkeys on them." She held up the pastry bag. "Gobble, gobble."

Jillian's gaze swept the kitchen. "Where's Bertie?"

"In the storeroom," Bertie said. "And if I were you, I'd start mixing up a batch of pumpkin cookies before she comes out."

"I made pumpkin cookies before I left," Jillian complained.

"And they're about all gone. You know Moss Hollow in November. Everyone goes pumpkin crazy. Besides, those cookies are *good*."

Jillian felt a mild glow at that last remark. It hadn't been that long that anyone called her baking efforts 'good.' She walked over to the recipe flip file and carried it to a table not far from Lenora. "What can you tell me about Gracie Mae Gonce?"

"Everybody went out to her restaurant. The food was good. Gracie Mae could certainly cook, though her taste in decor wasn't exactly my cup of tea."

"Cornelia liked it," Jillian said as she began gathering the ingredients for the cookies. Thankfully the things she needed were already in the kitchen from the morning batch so she didn't have to go into the storeroom. The longer she put off being scolded again by Bertie for her gallivanting around during work hours, the happier she would be.

"And I love Cornelia Montgomery to pieces," Lenora said, "but she can be right fond of all that froufrou stuff too. I'm more of a plain person. It makes everything so much easier to clean."

"About Gracie Mae, what did you think of her relationship with Bertie?" Jillian asked.

Lenora snorted. "Everybody knew about the feud between Gracie Mae and Bertie. It nearly drove Bertie to distraction, especially when Gracie Mae tried to copy all of The Chocolate Shoppe's top-selling sweets for her restaurant." She shook her head. "It wasn't right."

"She sounds almost deranged." Jillian scooped up flour for the cookies out of a deep bin, careful to dump it gently into the mixer so she didn't end up with a face full of it. "Did you know her husband or her son?"

Lenora squirted a glob of dark orange frosting on the cupcake in front of her. "I saw him around, but I don't think I probably exchanged a dozen words with him. The poor man drooped like a soggy scarecrow most of the time, and he'd flinch at loud noises. Folks used to say Wallace was the spitting image of Jack Harper, but I never saw the similarity myself."

Jillian smiled as a memory slipped through her mind of her grandfather teaching her how to drive a nail and the way he cheered her efforts, even in the face of a handful of bent nails. "Yeah, I don't ever remember Grandpa looking droopy."

Lenora chuffed a laugh at the thought. "Your grandfather was one of the cheeriest men I ever knew. He was always looking for something to do to help out."

"But Wallace Gonce didn't?"

"Not so I ever saw. He was a ghost haunting the real world. And that son of his made more of a splash, but not in a good way. Jack Gonce was always getting into trouble, throwing rocks through windows, shoplifting at Food for Less, and drinking." She shook her head. "That boy was wilder than a jack rabbit."

Jillian looked at Lenora in real surprise. "I heard my mom was interested in him at one point."

Lenora gave her a sad smile. "No one ever said your mama made good choices, honey. You have more sense in your little finger than your mama showed in her whole life—so far at least." She sniffed. "Imagine, running off and leaving a teenaged girl without her mama."

"I was a high school graduate with a job and a car." Jillian smiled at her. "Plus, I had Bertie and *you*. I wasn't exactly a pitiful orphan. Besides, she and Dad knew I'd be starting college in the fall."

Lenora harrumphed and turned back to her frosting turkeys. "Still wasn't right."

Jillian couldn't exactly argue with that. She turned her full attention back to her pumpkin cookies as she thought about Gracie Mae and her family. It seemed that she hadn't had a very happy life, and that unhappiness must have spilled over onto their son. She had enough life experience to know that the acting out behavior Lenora described could have come from trouble at home. Jillian wondered if she should expand her mental suspect pool to include the son. *If his mother made his father miserable, who did Jack side with?*

When Bertie came out of the storeroom, Jillian noticed her grandmother looked tired. The bakery stayed so busy and Jillian worried sometimes about Bertie's hard work and long hours. "Why don't you head on home?" she suggested. "Lenora and I can finish up here."

Bertie looked at Lenora who nodded. "Jillian is doing real well these days. We don't have that much to do. You go put your feet up."

"I suppose I'd be a fool to refuse the offer." She pointed at Jillian. "Don't forget to lock up tight."

"Lock up tight, got it."

Bertie narrowed her eyes. "And check the list for the bread orders tomorrow so we have all the ingredients out of the storeroom. It saves time in the mornings."

Jillian rolled her eyes. "I do know the drill. I've been working here for months."

Bertie folded her arms over her chest. "I know, but you can be forgetful when your head is full of that sleuthing foolishness. Which brings me to another question. Did you enjoy your late lunch?"

"Actually I skipped lunch and drove out to the Johnson farm."

And what did you learn out there?"

"Nothing," Jillian admitted. "Apparently Rascal wasn't home at the time of Gracie Mae's accident. He was out of town in Atlanta. His wife was home, but she died a couple years ago."

"I knew that," Bertie said. "I took them a casserole at the time. Darla Johnson was a good woman. And they have a fine son. Cancer is an awful thing."

Jillian certainly couldn't argue about that. She suddenly had a thought. "Speaking of sleuthing, I don't suppose you asked Byron about the loan for Gracie Mae."

Bertie harrumphed. "I did and after a big ol' long lecture about confidentiality, he finally admitted that he didn't have anything to be confidential about. Gracie Mae never took out a loan at the bank."

"Isn't that interesting," Jillian said.

"Annoying is more like it."

As she rolled out her cookie dough, Jillian watched her grandmother pull off her apron and get ready to go home. She always felt frightened whenever her vibrant grandmother looked tired. Jillian couldn't imagine what she would do if something happened to Bertie.

At the end of the day, Jillian tried to take joy in the fact that she hadn't burned a single cookie or misread any of the recipes she'd followed. She certainly was having more success with baking than sleuthing. She had no real clues and no idea of what to do next. She only hoped something would pop up.

After they closed the front and sent Maggie home, Lenora helped Jillian clean up the kitchen before heading to her apartment upstairs. Jillian paused at the back door, looking back at the neat, quiet kitchen. With the cooler outdoor temperatures, the kitchen was more bearable during the day, and Jillian felt she could learn to love the place. With that thought, she stepped outside and locked the door. Then she smacked herself in the forehead with the heel of her hand. She wasn't parked in the back lot. She'd need to walk around the block now to get to the tourist lot. *Oh well, the exercise will do me good*, she thought.

Night had fallen and the back alley was quite dark, lit only with a few poorly aimed security lights. Still, it was enough light to keep Jillian from falling into the holes dug by the city for whatever project they were doing to the side streets. Jillian hadn't thought to ask anyone what the point of all the digging actually was.

She skirted a fresh hole and picked up her pace. She knew once she got onto the main street that there would be a lot more streetlights, which would make her feel better. All she needed to round out her day would be to trip and fall.

She looked both ways quickly and started to cross the side street to reach the undamaged sidewalk on the other side. The long street appeared dark and still in both directions, but as soon as Jillian reached a third of the way across, bright car lights blinded her and she heard the hard revving of an engine as a car roared toward her.

Jillian screamed and froze for an instant in the blinding light. Someone was trying to run her over!

Jillian leaped for the curb, slamming to the ground with her feet still in the street. The car flashed past and the breeze of it stirred Jillian's clothes, but it didn't hit her. She drew her feet up out of the street, laying huddled for a moment, processing what had just happened—or what had almost happened. Thankfully whoever wanted to run her over didn't stick around for a second pass.

Jillian rolled painfully onto her rear and surveyed the damage. The palms of her hands stung as she fished her phone out of her pocket to call the police. While the phone rang, she looked down at the tears in her once snowy-white pants. She wondered which of the dark stains were from dirt and which were from bloody knees.

Since she was in the middle of town, it didn't take long for a sheriff's car to arrive. By then, Jillian had managed to stand, though her knees still felt shaky. She'd limped over to stand in the puddle of light from the closest streetlamp to pick at bits of gravel in her hands. When the door swung open on the car and Deputy Gooder Jones got out, Jillian groaned. *Perfect, totally perfect.*

"Are you all right?" Gooder asked, surprising Jillian. He actually sounded concerned.

"Scraped up, but I'm all right. I will probably be sore in the morning."

"I can drive you over to the clinic if you want to be checked out."

She shook her head. "I expect Bertie and Aunt Cornelia will doctor me when I get home. I'm afraid I didn't get a very good look at the car that tried to run me over, but I'm willing to bet it was driven by the same man who bid against Cornelia, broke into the storage unit office, and tried to break into Belle Haven."

Gooder held up his hands. "Whoa. Slow down with the conspiracy theories. Where did this hit and run attempt happen? Here on the corner?"

She pointed back up the darker side street. "I was crossing the street from the bakery alley so I could walk on the sidewalk."

"That street is pretty dark, and anyone driving it has to dodge a lot of construction," Gooder said. "Maybe some good ol' boy in a hurry to get home from work just didn't see you."

Jillian gestured at her white pants and light-colored coat. "Really? You don't think he saw me? I don't exactly fade into the shadows in this outfit. Do we have a lot of totally blind drivers in Moss Hollow? The car's lights went on, nearly blinding me. Then the car raced toward me. It was intentional."

"Or the guy turned out of one of the alleys, dodged the construction holes, and nearly ran you over, and you imagined the rest. Panic can lend a lot of spice to the imagination, and yours can be pretty spicy to begin with."

Jillian folded her arms over her chest and glared at him. "You have to be the most frustrating person I know. Are you not even going to make a report?"

Gooder pulled a pad out of his coat pocket. "Sure. Describe the vehicle."

"I told you, I didn't really see it. All I saw was headlights and I dove for the sidewalk."

"Was it definitely a car? Could it have been a truck?"

Jillian thought about it. "Maybe. Not a big truck, the lights weren't high enough, but it could have been a small pickup."

"Okay, so let me make sure we get all the details for the report. Directly across the alley from the bakery, you were almost hit by a vehicle that could have been any make of car or possibly a small truck. It's going to be a short report."

"At least it will be on record," Jillian said through gritted teeth.

Gooder flipped the notebook closed. "Good thing I love paperwork and standing out in the cold at night."

"Fine. Let's make it more purposeful. Did you know about Gracie Mae's car accident not long before she opened her restaurant?" Jillian asked.

"I knew about the car accident," Gooder said. "It's how her body was identified. I didn't know it was shortly before she opened the restaurant. She must have healed fast."

"Do you have any idea where she got the money for the restaurant? I understand her husband didn't have a great job, they didn't take out a loan, at least not locally, and she certainly didn't sue the deer for the accident."

Gooder took off his hat and ran his hand through his hair, staring off in the darkness for a moment. Then he reseated his hat and sighed before turning back to look at Jillian. "No, I don't know where she got the money. Maybe she'd been saving it in the sock drawer for years. Maybe she inherited it. Maybe Wallace inherited it. Maybe she robbed a bank for it. I don't know. I don't care. It's beyond my ability to bring her to justice if she got the money in some ill-gotten way because she's dead."

"I know she's dead. That's why this mysterious money ought to interest you."

"The car accident happened ten years before she was killed," Gooder said, his volume climbing. "Ten years. That's a little long for the two things to be linked."

"We've seen murder and attempted murder linked to events far more disparate than that," Jillian insisted.

"And that's the kind of wacky thinking that has you grasping at straws. Just because some outrageous thing happened once in an investigation doesn't mean I have to treat it as the new normal."

"Fine. I didn't really expect any help from you. Thanks for stopping by after my near-death experience." She turned and stomped off down the street toward the tourist lot.

"Drive carefully!" Gooder shouted after her.

"Thanks for your concern!" she shouted back.

"I'm not concerned." He was truly yelling. "I don't want to come back out in the cold!"

Jillian growled. She was tired of the whole business. She only wanted to get home.

Thankfully, the roads were fairly quiet because Jillian had a lot on her mind. Though it was still early evening, she felt tired and her hands and knees stung. The day had been too full and too frustrating. She wanted a nice quiet supper and maybe to curl up with a good book. She was tired of thinking when all her thoughts seemed to run around in circles.

She pulled in under the porte cochere and left her car there, suddenly too tired to deal with the longer walk from the garage. As she entered the kitchen, Bertie and Cornelia paused in the middle of cleaning up.

"You're certainly home late," Bertie said, then she seemed to take a really good look at Jillian. "What on earth did you do to your clothes?"

"Did you fall down?" Cornelia asked, walking around the counter to *tsk* over the stains on her coat and rips in her pants. "Are you all right?"

"I'm fine, but someone tried to run me over as I was crossing the street. I had to dive for the curb."

Bertie's glance flickered to the clock on the wall. "It's a little early for the Saturday night drink-and-drive accidents."

"I don't think it was an accident." Jillian leaned heavily on the counter. "I don't mind telling you about it, but I'm desperate for something hot to eat."

"I saved your plate in the oven," Cornelia said. "You wash up. And we should put something on your hands."

"I'll settle for washing the dirt out of them." Jillian walked over to the sink and winced as the soap and warm water poured over her scraped skin. After her hands were clean, she wet a paper towel and dabbed at her knees as Cornelia retrieved her plate from the oven and Bertie fixed her a cup of hot cocoa.

When Jillian was finally seated, she sipped the hot cocoa. She rarely drank the stuff, often finding it too sweet, but she always associated the drink with comfort. She remembered Bertie fixing her a cup on the day her parents pulled out of the driveway on their ridiculous journey to find themselves, leaving her behind at the age of eighteen. The same sweet beverage had appeared every time she suffered heartbreak or scraped knees while visiting her grandmother. She breathed in the sweet, rich scent and felt much of the stress of the day slip away.

"Eat your supper," Bertie said, pushing the plate with her finger. "You look pale."

Jillian laughed. "I'm a natural redhead. We're all pale." But she took a bite of the hot meatloaf on the plate and savored the comfort of it.

Cornelia and Bertie watched her patiently as she ate. Between bites Jillian described the blinding headlights and the car rushing out of nowhere at her. Finally she pushed the empty plate away.

Picking up the plate, Bertie carried it to the kitchen counter. "So then what did you do?"

"I called the police, of course, but Gooder thinks I imagined about half of it."

"Gooder Jones has his moments of competence," Bertie said, "but he can be a real nincompoop."

Jillian laughed. That was a word she didn't hear very often. "It hasn't been a particularly productive day. I wish I could find out more about Gracie Mae's car accident. Laura Lee told me the details of the accident report made it sound as if there could have been two cars there. But Gracie Mae insisted she ran off the road to avoid a deer and there were no other cars around."

"You drove out there," Bertie said. "You saw that curve out in front of the farm. It's a wonder more people don't plow into trees there, especially this time of year when the deer seem to be everywhere looking for food. The other tracks could have been from another car that swerved to avoid a different deer, but didn't hit anything. Then they didn't need to call the police. The two tracks may have nothing to do with one another."

"It's a pretty big coincidence," Jillian said dryly.

Bertie shrugged. "I've seen bigger. I'm only saying we don't know that all those tire tracks happened at the same time."

Jillian took a sip from her cooling mug to cover her annoyance. She didn't appreciate hearing Bertie blow off her concerns. After all, she was trying to make the connections so that the police would have somewhere to look for Gracie Mae's killer, somewhere that didn't involve Bertie. She set the mug carefully on the table. "Did anyone say anything today about the murder?"

"Not to me directly." Bertie looked away, one of the sure signs she was trying to avoid saying something.

"But folks aren't exactly subtle when they gossip, are they?" Jillian asked.

Bertie's gaze turned back to her and sharpened. "Not exactly. Look, we've all had a long day, and I'm ready to forget about this whole murder business. Let the authorities figure it out." She got up and started across the room. She paused at the doorway and turned back to Jillian. "I wish you'd be more careful."

"Says the woman who nagged Byron into telling her about bank loans," Jillian said.

"You'll notice that no one tried to run me down afterward. I'd hoped to get the answer to the question about the money, so you wouldn't keep poking around. Any time you get one of these bees in your bonnet, things get hairy around here."

Jillian blinked, sorting out the mixed metaphor. Her grandmother turned and walked through the doorway. As Jillian watched Bertie go, she puzzled over her grandmother's behavior. Normally Bertie believed in standing up, digging in, even making a scene. The woman who just wanted to wash her hands of it confused and worried her. She started when Cornelia's blue-veined hand rested on her wrist.

"Be patient with Bertie. She never really understood Gracie Mae's fixation on her, and all this brings up some more painful times in her past." She looked in the direction her sister had gone. "And I expect it makes her miss Jack all the more. You know your grandmother could have remarried after your grandfather died. Plenty of men were still interested in her."

Jillian knew that Bertie could still catch the interest of some of the older men in town. She'd seen enough evidence of that. "She thinks she's too old."

Cornelia snorted. "She says that, but she doesn't think it. Bertie Harper won't consider herself old until Death comes knocking and carries her off kicking and screaming. She never looked at another man because Jack Harper was *that* important to her. Same as Raymond was to me."

"I wish she'd talk to me."

"Well, if wishes were horses then beggars would ride. But there is someone you *can* talk to about Gracie Mae."

Jillian sat up straighter. "Who?"

"Estelle," Cornelia said. "You'll see her in the morning. She plays the organ and the piano at church."

Jillian's brown wrinkled. "Estelle Morgan?"

"Estelle Gonce Morgan. Wallace Gonce's little sister."

Jillian sat back in her seat, astonished at how her options had turned so quickly. She smiled at her great-aunt. "Do you think she'll talk to me?"

"I don't know. Estelle is in my garden club, but I don't know her terribly well. I do know she isn't much of a gossip, but I remember thinking several times that she didn't care for her sister-in-law much. It wasn't in her words. It was in her body language whenever Gracie Mae was around. Though her beef was probably mostly over how sad Wallace always looked, she still might be willing to tell you any dirt she knows. Especially since Gracie Mae is dead, so it's not as if gossip can hurt her."

"It still sounds like I should tread carefully."

Cornelia picked up Jillian's scraped hand. "Sweetheart, I'd say treading carefully might be all that keeps you alive."

11

Jillian woke up aching. *I can't believe diving onto the sidewalk could make me hurt this much.* The skin on her scabbed-over knees felt tight as well, and she shuffled to the bathroom for her shower hoping the hot water would help loosen everything up.

By the time she made it down to breakfast, she could walk without limping or wincing. The heady scent of bacon and maple syrup met her as she reached the kitchen. "French toast," Cornelia sang out from where she stood at the electric griddle. "I thought we all needed something special to brighten the day."

Bertie didn't comment but she did hand Jillian a steaming mug of coffee before turning back to her bacon. Jillian thanked her and took a restorative sip. She opened her mouth to speak and Bertie held up a hand. "I'm setting a rule for this morning. It's Sunday and I don't want any murder or investigation talk. Got it?"

"Got it. I was going to say that the bacon smelled fantastic."

Bertie's mouth quirked. "I do believe in going to church on a good breakfast. If more people did that we'd have less stomach growling."

Cornelia laughed. "Amen to that. Did you hear Bill Lytle's stomach last Sunday? It sounded like he'd smuggled in a bear cub."

The almost smile on Bertie's face twitched. "I didn't notice. I was too busy wondering if Ginny Plover was going to die of embarrassment or starvation. Every time her stomach roared, the poor thing turned as red as Christmas."

"Well, not everyone has the best cooks in Moss Hollow making breakfast," Jillian said. "By the way, I may be a little late for the Sweetie Pies meeting for reasons I am forbidden to discuss per your rule."

Bertie's face clouded up. "No. I'm serious, young lady. We don't need to let this investigation foolishness take over our lives. The Sweetie Pies meet at our bakery and we're *all* going to be there as hosts."

She glared at Jillian until she stammered a "Yes, ma'am." Jillian was absolutely going to talk to Estelle, but she'd have to be sure it didn't interfere with the baking club meeting.

Though the church service was as good as always with a wonderful message about community, Jillian found her nerves taunt. At one point, Bertie poked her in the side. "Stop fidgeting."

Jillian wondered if it was her day to feel like a wayward ten-year-old; perhaps that was the risk she ran for living with her grandmother. When the service ended, Jillian slipped away before Bertie could scold her for anything else. She walked up the center aisle, smiling and shaking hands with people as she went. She managed to reach the organ while Estelle was still packing up her music. "The music today certainly was beautiful," Jillian said.

Estelle patted the organ. "I'm blessed to be able to work with such a fine instrument." Then she looked at Jillian and raised an eyebrow. "But you didn't really come up here to praise my playing."

Does every older woman in Moss Hollow have mind-reading skills? Jillian felt her cheeks warm, but she fessed up. "I actually have something I need to talk to you about."

Estelle hugged her packet of music to her chest. "Something about my sister-in-law?"

"Okay, that's spooky," Jillian said.

Estelle smiled. "Not so much. I heard about you finding Gracie Mae's bones. All these years I thought she'd run off and left my brother."

"So you knew she was missing."

"Of course. She was family. What kind of Christian would I be if I didn't even notice my brother's wife never seemed to be around when I visited?"

"But your brother never filed a missing person's report."

Estelle's gaze turned to the beautiful church sanctuary and the tall stained glass windows and her jaw tightened as she pressed her lips together. "I don't want to talk about that woman in here. Come to my house this afternoon, and I'll tell you what I know."

Jillian tentatively suggested a time that would let her get through the baking club meeting first. She felt a rush of relief when Estelle agreed. Then the older woman swept by Jillian and down the side aisle of the church, her posture rigidly erect. She seemed even angrier at Gracie Mae than Bertie, and Bertie was the one who was supposedly in the middle of a feud. Feeling suddenly confident that Sunday was going to be far more successful than Saturday, Jillian headed off to find her grandmother and aunt so she could take them out to eat.

They caught Sunday brunch at the Southern Peach Inn and Jillian continued to honor Bertie's ban on investigative talk until the end of the meal when her grandmother looked at her pointedly. "What did you want with Estelle today?"

"Can't tell you," Jillian said, putting on her most innocent expression. "Just following your rule."

"You know, there are moments when I agree with Gooder Jones," Bertie grumbled. "You can be intentionally annoying."

"Fine. I want to find out if she knows why Wallace didn't file a missing person's report when his wife was clearly missing."

Bertie thought about it for a moment. "A reasonable question, but don't make a nuisance of yourself. Estelle Morgan is a fine woman."

"I wasn't going to flog her. I want to know what she knows. And I'm not sure it's going to be that hard to find out. She clearly wasn't fond of Gracie Mae."

Cornelia set her glass of sweet tea on the table. "Not surprising. She was Wallace's sister and Gracie Mae was horrible to the man."

"So everyone assumes," Bertie said. "But I never saw her do anything to him."

"True," Cornelia said as she folded her hands neatly on the very edge of the table. "She mostly acted as if he didn't exist. What husband wouldn't love that?"

"The man could have stood up for himself," Bertie grumbled.

"Maybe. All I know is that I never saw the poor fellow happy."

Bertie tossed her napkin on the table. "We should be going. I need to put on the coffee for the Sweetie Pies meeting. I don't remember who is responsible for treats this week."

"Savannah," Jillian said, stunned for once to be more on top of things than her grandmother. She wondered if that was a reflection of how stressed Bertie was from recent events.

Once they got to the bakery, Bertie's tense posture relaxed, and she bustled around getting the front ready for the meeting. She commanded Jillian to push the tables together so the group could sit comfortably. Jillian, who had already been in the middle of that very activity, refrained from saying anything, She was happy to see her grandmother looking more her normal, bossy self.

When the club meeting finally got started, Jillian nibbled on one of Savannah's cranberry pecan cookies and thought of how much she appreciated autumn cookie time. As soon as the introductory business was over, every eye turned toward her.

"So?" Maudie said. "Are you going to fill us in?"

"There isn't much going on," Jillian said hesitantly. "This is a police matter now."

Laura Lee laughed out loud at that. "When has that ever kept you from asking questions and poking around?" She leaned forward and looked at Jillian intently. "And don't think I don't see the scrapes on your hands. Gooder said you were almost run over."

Gasps around the table showed this was news to most of the club. Lenora smacked a broad hand down on the wood of the table, making everyone jump. "This is getting ridiculous. You're like my own daughter, except you don't drive me nearly as crazy. I don't want to see you hurt."

"The best way to do that is to solve this murder," Jillian said. "Once we know who killed Gracie Mae, we'll know who tried to run me over."

"I knew trying to run you over wasn't going to stop you," Wanda Jean said in an approving tone. "So what's your next move?"

"Well," Jillian said. "I'm going to talk to Estelle Gonce Morgan this afternoon. I want to know why Wallace didn't file a missing person's report."

"I want to know that myself," Laura Lee said. "I know Gooder talked to her. She doesn't know where her brother is living. She lost track of him about six months ago."

Jillian perked up. This was news. "Does she know why?"

"If she does, Gooder didn't say," Laura Lee said. "I'll be interested to hear what you find out."

"So will I," Maudie said.

"Estelle is a nice lady," Savannah said. "I helped her out with her taxes last year. She's reserved, but gracious. And she's a wonder with a crochet hook. I've never seen so many doilies as she has in her front parlor. You should be sure to check out her afghans at the church Christmas bazaar."

Jillian wished she were more crafty or musical, as either might give her a point of connection with Estelle.

"I know Estelle pretty well," Maudie said. "She was teaching me to crochet some years back, before my aching hands made it too hard. I know she didn't like her sister-in-law one bit. She fretted over her brother. She said she believed his wife up and leaving him were a big part in destroying his health."

"Wallace wasn't well?" Bertie interrupted.

"Apparently not," Maudie replied, her tone slightly tart. Jillian knew she hated being interrupted. "I don't know what was wrong with him though. Estelle can get a bit carried away, but she tends to clam up if you ask for details, and then she always insists that she's no gossip." Maudie, who adored gossip, sniffed in offense as she recalled the remark.

By the end of the meeting, they hadn't conducted much baking club business, but they'd analyzed Estelle and her family relationships as thoroughly as possible. Finally Wanda Jean stood up and announced it was time to adjourn.

"Since when are you so hot to dash off?" Bertie demanded. "You and Maudie usually hang around until the last cat's hung."

Maudie gave her best friend a sly sideways glance then mock whispered, "It's because Wanda Jean has a boyfriend."

Wanda Jean stiffened. "I certainly do not. You know I have no interest in adding a man to my life. My late husband was a good man, and I don't need another."

"Sure," Maudie said. "So why are you so gussied up?"

Jillian looked over Wanda Jean's neatly tailored skirt and ultra-feminine silken blouse with ruffles and a soft floral pattern. It was unusually dressy for Wanda Jean, whose taste in clothes tended to resemble Bertie's. Also, as Wanda Jean turned her head to glare at her best friend, Jillian noticed that the old fashioned thick knot she normally twisted her hair into had been replaced with a softer chignon.

"I'm certainly not going to entertain this silly topic," Wanda Jean snapped. "I have an appointment." She turned and stomped out of the bakery with Maudie's cackling laugh following her.

"You shouldn't tease," Cornelia scolded Maudie. "Wanda Jean is still young. I think it's good if she's shown an interest in a man."

Though Wanda Jean was pushing sixty, Jillian agreed that was well young enough to enjoy the company of a new man in her life. She would have stayed to defend her, but Jillian had her own appointment to get to, so she left the meeting with the sound of laughter and teasing following her out.

The drive to Estelle's house didn't take long as she lived not far from the church. Her little ranch house was almost lost in the trees that filled the older woman's yard, throwing shadows that made the weak autumn sun struggle to reach the house's front door. Jillian pulled to the curb and walked up to the door. Since the house had no doorbell, she knocked and waited, hearing the sound of a little dog barking somewhere inside.

After a few minutes Jillian knocked again, rapping as firmly as her sore hands would allow, but still got no answer. She turned the side of her hand and pounded, wondering if Estelle might have laid down for an afternoon nap, but surely the dog barking would have wakened her.

As she was wondering what to do next, a small brown dog raced around the side of the house and barked noisily at Jillian. Jillian bent over slightly and spoke to the yapping animal. "Where's your master?"

The little dog rushed up to her, making Jillian jump. It grabbed the loose leather of Jillian's slouchy boots and tugged, then raced toward the side of the house, yapping away. Though the tiny animal was hardly Lassie, Jillian thought it was pretty clear the little dog wanted her to follow.

She walked around the side of the house and saw the gate to the tall wooden fence that surrounded the backyard was latched closed, but the ground was dug out underneath it. The dog gave Jillian one last volley of yaps, then ducked through the gap. Jillian opened the gate latch and walked into the backyard just in time to see the little dog race through a doggie flap in the back door.

Jillian walked up to the back door and knocked as she shifted back and forth trying to get a view inside through the narrow curtains that covered the back door window. She could see that the door opened into the kitchen. Then she froze in shock as her gaze travelled to the floor and she glimpsed two stocking-clad legs barely visible behind the counter. The little dog put his paws on the legs to brace for the jump over them.

The legs never moved.

J illian rattled the doorknob and smacked the glass of the window with the flat of her hand. "Estelle! Mrs. Morgan!" The legs didn't even twitch. While she fished her phone from her jacket pocket, she turned and looked around for something heavy enough to break the window.

When the emergency operator picked up on the other end of her call, Jillian babbled into the phone, barely able to follow the operator's line of thought to answer the questions. She was fairly certain she gave the right address before she simply hung up. She needed all her attention on getting into the house. She stepped off the back patio, still searching for something to break the window. She thought of all the times she'd seen people break windows on television with their elbows, but decided she didn't want to join Estelle on a trip to the emergency room.

Finally she spotted something gray under a shrub and pounced on what appeared to be a good-sized stone. It turned out to be a key holder with a key inside. Whispering a prayer of thanks all the while, Jillian fished out the key and opened the back door.

The legs indeed belonged to Estelle Morgan. The woman lay as still as death with a huge lump on her head and blood caked in her hair. Jillian knelt beside her and pressed her fingers to Estelle's neck. The skin was warm and she felt an encouragingly strong pulse under her fingers. Estelle was unconscious, but alive.

Weak-kneed from relief, Jillian slid down the nearby cabinets and sat on the floor near Estelle. She wasn't sure what to do. Should she elevate the organist's head or her feet? Feet was for shock, she was pretty sure of that. Since she wasn't sure of the right procedure and felt a burst of terror whenever she thought of accidentally making the woman's condition worse, she simply sat on the floor and waited for the ambulance to arrive.

The little dog walked over and looked up at Jillian with slightly bulgy eyes. she was so close to the little animal that Jillian could see the dog was female with fur thickly covered with dirt. "Digging out from under the fence must have been some job, huh girl?"

The dog wagged her tail enthusiastically. Then she went back to her mistress's side and settled down with her head on her tiny paws. It was as if she realized all they could do was wait.

Jillian looked around the kitchen, or as much as she could see of it from her spot on the floor. The floor was immaculate. Bertie and Cornelia both believed firmly in cleanliness being next to godliness, but Jillian doubted there was a floor in Belle Haven that could match Estelle's for sterility. Fascinated by the almost impossible cleanliness, Jillian scooted closer to the fridge. Surely the gap between the fridge and the counter would be a little dirty. Nope. She stuck her finger into the space and felt only the perfect smoothness of the tile.

"Judging by this floor, Estelle would freak out if she saw you so muddy," Jillian said to the dog. The little dog responded with tail wagging but didn't stand. As Jillian's gaze continued to sweep the room in fascination, she spotted something decidedly out of place. Jillian crawled over for a closer look and found a torn piece of dark fabric. She picked it up and ran the ragged fabric between her fingers. It was light, but sturdy, probably pants fabric. With Estelle's obvious cleanliness bug, how had a piece of fabric been overlooked?

Before she could ponder it further, Jillian heard pounding on the front door. Of course, it must be locked. Shoving the scrap of fabric into her pocket, she scrambled to her feet and hurried through the house. She flung open the door so the emergency workers could rush in and then led them briskly to the kitchen.

The little dog offered the new strangers a single yap before Jillian scooped her up and backed away to give them room to work. "Don't worry," she whispered to the muddy dog. "They'll take good care of Estelle."

The portly young man who seemed to be in charge fired questions at Jillian. "How long has Estelle been on the floor? Does she have a history of light-headedness? Is she diabetic? Has she been ill?" For every question, Jillian had no answer.

Finally the questions stopped when it was obvious that Jillian would have no helpful answers. Then Gooder Jones showed up. The deputy walked into the kitchen and fired off his own questions at the emergency workers. Estelle was still unconscious, the result of a hard blow to the head, but they had no idea where the blow came from.

"Could she have fallen and hit her head?" Gooder asked.

"Sure, but our job is to get her to the hospital, not figure out how she got on the floor."

Gooder harrumphed, then turned his scowl toward Jillian. "Why is it that whenever something awful happens in Moss Hollow, I can count on your attendance at the scene?"

"Just lucky I guess." She hugged the dog to her chest and looked past the deputy to Estelle as she was loaded onto a stretcher. She still showed no sign of consciousness.

"What brought you out here?" Gooder asked. "You a friend of Mrs. Morgan?"

Jillian shook her head. "I don't really know her. She plays the organ really well, but you know that." Jillian had seen Gooder at church, though his attendance appeared to be sporadic.

He bobbed his head. "So why are you here?"

Jillian looked directly into the deputy's eyes. "She's Gracie Mae Gonce's sister-in-law. I wanted to ask her if she knew why Wallace never filed a missing person's report for Gracie Mae."

"And how would you know that?"

She ignored the question. "Don't you find it coincidental that I made an appointment to chat with Estelle, and when I get here, she is on the floor unconscious?"

"Who did you tell about your appointment?"

"The members of the Sweetie Pies."

He perked up at that. "Including your grandmother?"

"Oh, come on," she said, her volume rising. "You cannot believe Bertie Harper raced over here and bopped that woman on the head. Bertie would be pleased you think she's so spry."

He stared at her for a long moment, then backed down. "No, I don't. I think people Estelle's age fall down sometimes and whack their heads. My great-aunt Nora fell and broke a hip last month. Falls happen. I don't see a big deal here."

"I'm sorry about your aunt," Jillian said, "but I don't believe Estelle just happened to fall a couple hours before she was going to talk to me about Gracie Mae's disappearance."

"Actually, she probably did. Timing for accidents can be inconvenient that way. That's one reason they're called accidents."

Jillian rolled her eyed. "Are you aware that Estelle really disliked Gracie Mae? Apparently she was uncharacteristically passionate about it."

"So? I'm not so fond of you, but I've managed to avoid murdering you, if that's what you're implying about Estelle. I've known the woman since I was a kid. She isn't the sort to kill her sister-in-law."

"But you believe Bertie is?"

"Your grandmother is feisty." He held up a hand before Jillian could begin yelling at him. "But no. I don't think Bertie killed anyone or is in danger of killing anyone. I still don't know how Gracie Mae Gonce died. It could have been an accident, the same as Estelle's fall today."

"I hope you're at least going to keep Estelle safe," Jillian said. "In case her accident wasn't so accidental."

"The hospital has security. She'll be fine." He pointed at Jillian. "One thing I do not want to hear is that you're telling people that someone in Moss Hollow is conking little old ladies on the head. You'll start a panic."

"Maybe folks need to be a little panicky."

"I'll lock you up as a public menace."

"I'd like to see you try."

They both glared at one another for a long moment, then Gooder threw his hands into the air and declared, "You're hopeless."

Since the subject of Estelle's attack was clearly pointless, Jillian held up the little dog. "What happens to the dog?"

"That dog?"

"Do you see any other dogs?"

"It's not my problem. I'll call animal control. They can pick it up."

Jillian was horrified at that idea. The little dog had gone through a lot to get help for Estelle. She may have saved the organist's life. Jillian couldn't handle the thought of the poor little thing alone and shivering at the animal shelter. "You don't need to do that. I'll look after the dog until Estelle is well enough to get her back."

"Suit yourself."

"I'll need to collect some supplies," Jillian said. "Dog food and such. I'll need to open cupboards for that."

"I don't suppose Estelle would mind, and apparently she invited you over. This isn't a crime scene as far as I can tell. Let me shoot a few pictures, just in case, then you're welcome to look for the dog stuff and go home."

Jillian swallowed down the snarky remark and stood out of the way while Gooder snapped photos. Then she opened cabinets until she found the dog's food, some dishes, and a leash. As before, she was struck by how perfectly organized the cupboards and drawers were. It reminded her of the pretend kitchens at home renovation stores.

She thought of the scrap of cloth in her pocket and turned to look at Gooder who was taking photos of the back door lock. He would almost surely blow off the clue, but he might take it with him. Then she wouldn't have it. Not that she had any idea what to do with it. She couldn't exactly picture herself matching it to pants all over Moss Hollow like some crazy character from Cinderella.

Finally she decided to hold on to the clue for the moment. She gathered up the food and snapped the leash on the dog's collar. "Let's go home, well, my home anyway." The little dog looked up at her with its buggy eyes, and Jillian hoped the little thing would be able to come back home again soon.

When Jillian got to Belle Haven, Bertie was about as thrilled to see the dog as Jillian could have predicted. "Do you have any idea how much trouble dogs are?" her grandmother demanded when she met Jillian in the front foyer. "They aren't convenient the way cats are. You have to walk them. And they chew on things."

Jillian shrugged. "And Possum upchucks hairballs and eats house plants. Besides, the dog won't be staying all that long."

"Is that what you're going to call it?" Bertie asked. "The dog?"

"It don't know her name."

"Her name is Angel."

They turned to look at Cornelia as she swept into the room like a Gothic heroine. She had changed from the muted floral dress she'd worn to church into something filmy and dark.

"What are you wearing?" Bertie said.

"I am trying out some new choices for communing with the spirit world," Cornelia said. "I ordered this from an online store. I find online shopping quite interesting. They sent me a sage stick. I'm thinking it'll come in handy for the turkey stuffing this year."

Jillian almost laughed at that. For all her talk about the Belle Haven haint, the ghost that was supposed to haunt the old house, Cornelia really had very little interest in the weirder practices of ghost hunting. "I thought you were into smudging?"

"I tried it," Cornelia admitted, "when the filmmakers were here. But it annoyed my sinuses and left poor Raymond sneezing for a week."

"Speaking of," Bertie said, "where is Possum? We should probably keep him separate from Angel. We know how he can be."

As if conjured up by the mention of his name, Possum raced into the room and skidded to a stop in front of the little dog. The two stared at one another for a moment and Jillian tensed to snatch up Angel before the cat could scratch her eyes out. To her shock, instead of violence, the two sniffed noses and then Possum began licking the dog's matted fur.

"Personal grooming was always very important to Raymond," Cornelia said. She wrinkled her nose as she looked at the dog. "Estelle would be quite horrified if she saw the state of her little dog. It's normally white."

"How do you know?"

"Estelle brings Angel to garden club meetings sometimes."

"If you're going to keep the dog for now, you should wash it," Bertie said. "I don't need mud all over the house."

And so Jillian ended up in the laundry room washing the tiny dog in the sink. As Cornelia had said, the fur under the caked-on dirt was snowy white except for dark tracks at the corners of the dog's eyes. Nothing Jillian could do seemed to get that clean. Still, as she dried Angel with a towel, Jillian had to admit that the dog had undergone quite a transformation. Her fur dried to a soft white fluff.

Jillian's memory of the remarkable cleanliness of Estelle's house, along with her frustration at not getting any of her questions answered, sent Jillian on a cleaning frenzy throughout the downstairs. She dusted and mopped. Angel was clearly used to such behavior as she did a good job at staying out of the way except when she needed to go outside, which seemed to be often.

Jillian was glad the weather outside was so pleasant when she led the little dog outside yet again. "You're just a giant water balloon, aren't you?"

Angel wagged her tail in reply and pranced across the back lawn. Early evening shadows spread toward the house from the woods even though Jillian's watch said it was still afternoon. The shortening of the days in autumn was the one thing she didn't care much for. Angel tugged the leash, pulling Jillian closer and closer to the tree line.

"Can't you go already?" Jillian asked. "Why do you have to find the perfect grass for it?"

To her surprise, the dog suddenly launched into a flurry of high-pitched yaps and jerked at the leash. "Hold on," Jillian said. "We're not going back there. I don't care how many possums you smell."

The dog pulled harder, still barking. Then she flipped around so that she was facing Jillian and began backing up, tugging at the leash. "What are you doing?"

The dog was clearly smarter than Jillian expected. She lowered her head while she pulled against the leash and the collar simply popped over her head. Free of the leash, the dog dashed into the shadowy overgrown part of the garden, leaving Jillian holding an empty collar dangling at the end of the pink leash.

"Angel! Get back here!" Jillian yelled the dog's name over and over as she hurried through the nearly dark portion of the back garden. She tried not to imagine the small animal confronting something wild with teeth and possibly rabies. *A great dog sitter I am.*

At least the constant yapping gave Jillian a direction to follow. The yaps, now interspersed with growls, grew more furious. Jillian held her breath, hoping whatever Angel had found wouldn't hurt her too badly. Then, to her shock, she heard a very human shout, then a yelp.

"Leave that dog alone!" Jillian bellowed as she picked up speed. She reached the clearing where the old fountain stood, clogged with lichen and muck. The little dog lay panting under the fountain. "Angel?"

To Jillian's vast relief, Angel hopped to her feet and picked up something on the ground beside her. She limped toward Jillian with the thing hanging limply from her mouth.

Jillian bent and scooped up the dog. She could see another torn scrap of cloth clenched in Angel's teeth and gently pulled it free. In the shadows of the overgrown garden, the scrap was a match to the one she'd found at Estelle's house. Apparently Estelle's attacker had followed them home.

Jillian hugged the little dog close to her and spun in a slow circle, peering into the deep shadows. Is the person who killed Gracie Mae lurking out there, waiting to bash me in the head? She began walking back toward the house, pausing repeatedly to turn and look in every direction, but she couldn't shake the panic building inside her that whoever had kicked the dog could burst out of the shadows at any moment and go after her as well. Finally she gave in to the feeling and ran for the house.

As soon as she came through the back door, she locked it behind her. It was still late afternoon, but Jillian intended no more walks in the poorly lit backyard. "You'll simply have to water the grass out front," she whispered to the little dog in her arms.

Carefully she lowered the dog to the floor and squatted beside her. "Where did the bad man kick you?"

Angel licked her hands enthusiastically, and didn't whimper or growl as Jillian ran her hands over the dog's legs and paws, then over her body. Jillian walked to the fridge to sneak Angel a little bit of Aunt Cornelia's bacon stash, normally reserved for Possum. Angel followed her and Jillian could again see the dog was limping slightly. She tore off the end of a piece of bacon and handed it to Angel who gobbled it down enthusiastically.

"My, the house looks nice and smells of lemon," Aunt Cornelia said as she walked into the kitchen. "What brought on the cleaning frenzy?"

"Probably seeing the sterile operating theater that Estelle lives in." Jillian pointed at the little dog. "Watch Angel walk. Do you think I should take her to the vet?"

Cornelia called Angel and the dog scampered over to her, still visibly limping. "She wasn't limping earlier."

"No, she had an encounter outside." Jillian explained about the dog's rush into the darkness and the yelp, as well as the sound of a man shouting. She pulled the matching scraps of fabric from her pocket. "Do these look the same to you?"

Cornelia walked over and took the two fabrics, rubbing them between her fingers. "I would say yes." She turned to look out the tall windows on the wall of the breakfast room. Darkness pressed against them, revealing nothing beyond. "Do you think you and Angel scared him off?"

"I have no idea," Jillian said.

"Have you called the police? It seems they would want to know about this."

Jillian groaned. "I am not sure Gooder wants to know anything about anything. He didn't listen to me at all earlier, why should he do so now?"

Cornelia held up her hand with the scraps of fabric. "You have something tangible here."

"You haven't seen how good Gooder is at ignoring things."

"He does seem to be a stubborn young man. It's enough to make me wonder if we're related."

Jillian winced. "That's a charming thought."

"Well, if you're not going to call the police this evening, promise you'll take this evidence in tomorrow. You can always hand it over to Laura Lee. She seems a level-headed sort."

"That brings me back to Angel," Jillian said. "Should I take her over to the vet?"

Cornelia looked down at the little dog, who responded to the attention with tail wagging. "I don't think this warrants emergency attention, but I think you should take her to Dr. West in the morning." Doctor Shane West was Possum's vet.

Jillian nodded. "I feel comfortable with that. Now, I'm going to go make sure all the doors and windows are locked. Then I think I'll clean some bathrooms."

"I would tell you not to worry so much, but who am I to stand in the way of cleaning? Scrub on!"

Though cleaning freed her mind to think about the events of the past days, Jillian had to admit that the only thing she had really accomplished was finally getting the grout in her bathroom looking snow white again. Angel grew bored of watching her and ended up napping in a pile with her new buddy, Possum.

On Monday morning, Jillian woke to the smell of flowers and realized it was the shampoo she'd used on Angel. The little dog was curled into a tight ball on the pillow beside her. When Angel saw Jillian was awake, she popped up and lapped the end of Jillian's nose with her pink tongue.

"Good morning to you too," Jillian said as she sat up to get her face out of licking range. "I hope you're feeling better."

The little dog raced to the end of the bed, hopped down onto the blanket chest and then to the floor, which answered the question of how the little ball of fluff had gotten on the bed in the first place. Angel stopped at the bedroom door and barked.

"Right. You want a walk." Jillian grabbed her robe from a nearby chair. "Just when I was beginning to think I enjoyed having a dog."

They went out the front door, and Jillian shivered slightly in her robe. The day was unusually chilly for November in Georgia. "If you want to hurry," she told the dog, "I'm in favor."

As far as she could tell, Angel paid her no attention at all, sniffing every bush until apparently her little bladder couldn't hold out any longer and she finally attended to business. The warmth of the house when Jillian stepped back inside was like a hug. She unsnapped Angel's leash and walked to the kitchen with the little dog at her side.

As often happened, Cornelia and Bertie were already in the breakfast room. Bertie put down the coffee mug she'd been holding and looked over the edge of the table. "Cornelia said Angel was injured. She looks all right."

"She is barely limping today," Jillian agreed. "I still want to run by Dr. West's office and have him take a look at her. I feel responsible since she isn't my dog."

Bertie raised her coffee mug to her lips and blew across the dark beverage. "Seems reasonable."

"I also want to run by the sheriff's office and have Laura Lee look at the scraps of cloth, so I'm going to be late to the bakery."

"No problem," Bertie said, though her tone didn't quite match her words. "Lenora and I can handle the pre-Thanksgiving rush just fine."

"You know what that's called?" Cornelia asked as she spread peach jam on a warm biscuit. "Passive-aggressive. That's when you say something that sounds positive but is really meant to make the person feel guilty."

Bertie narrowed her eyes at her sister. "You've been watching afternoon talk shows again."

"They've very educational, and it gives me something to look at while I'm up in my crafting room."

"Oh?" Jillian said, hoping to turn the conversation from both her guilt and talk shows. "What are you working on?"

"I'm tatting snowflakes for the Christmas bazaar." Cornelia bit a tiny nibble from the edge of her biscuit. Jillian often marveled at her great-aunt's ability to eat while making no mess at all. She didn't believe in Cornelia's ghost talk, but she was completely capable of seeing that one trick as almost magical.

"Well, if you're going to run all those errands, you best eat up and get about it then," Bertie insisted, jerking Jillian from her reverie and back to the task of gobbling down the best biscuits in Moss Hollow.

At the vet's office, Dr. West recognized Angel right away and he turned concerned eyes toward Jillian. "I heard about Estelle's fall. How is she doing?"

"I don't know," Jillian admitted. "I haven't heard."

The vet nodded as he rubbed Angel's ears. "So what's ailing Angel?"

Jillian explained about the intruder in the Belle Haven gardens. "I didn't see him, but I suspect he kicked her."

"That's appalling." The vet began gently probing the dog's limbs. "Any man that would kick a little thing like Angel should get a good swift kick of his own."

"I'm with you on that."

Finally Dr. West found a tender spot, making Angel wince but not yelp or growl. "I'm pretty sure this is just a bruise. No serious damage."

Jillian let out a relieved huff. "I'm so glad."

"You know, we offer a kennel service for our patients. Angel has stayed with us before. If you want to leave her, she's welcome here."

Jillian considered the offer, but was surprised to find she didn't want to hand over the little dog. "Thanks so much," she said, "but

I've gotten attached to this little hero. I think we'll look after her until Estelle is well."

"I don't blame you. Angel is a sweetheart." Then he waved away Jillian's offer to pay the bill and she left the office. Not for the first time, she thought of how very special Moss Hollow could be sometimes.

As soon as she'd popped Angel into Possum's pet carrier, Jillian called Laura Lee to tell her she was coming by to give her something.

"Something fun like a Chocolate Shoppe pastry or something I'm not going to enjoy at all?"

Jillian winced. "More the second." She told her friend about the two scraps of cloth.

Laura Lee whistled. "You are going to give Gooder Jones a stroke one of these days. I can't believe you didn't hand that over at the scene and you didn't call in an intruder."

"I never saw the intruder," Jillian said in her defense, "though Angel did."

"Well come on over with the fabric, but you might want to keep the whole pastry as a bribe in mind."

The more Jillian thought about the pastry bribe, the more she thought it sounded like a pretty good idea. She drove over to the bakery and pulled up out front, hauling the pet carrier along with her. There was a line for the cash register so Jillian set the pet carrier on the floor near the counter and slipped behind, grabbing a pair of latex gloves from the box so she could serve herself.

Maggie looked sideways at her. "Is it 'bring your cat to work' day?"

"Dog," Jillian said as she began loading a box with pastries. "And we're just passing through."

"You'd better be."

Jillian jumped at the sharp sound of her grandmother's voice, knocking her head against the edge of the counter. "Ow."

"What are you doing?" Bertie asked.

"Taking a bribe to the sheriff's department," Jillian answered. "Can I leave Angel here while I run over there? I don't want to give Gooder anything new to fuss about."

"No. This is a bakery, not a kennel. Take the dog back to Belle Haven."

Jillian wasn't about to drive all the way back to the house then to the sheriff's department, but she knew better than to argue with Bertie. "No problem."

Bertie harrumphed and stomped back into the kitchen.

Maggie leaned close to Jillian. "You missed the really good stuff."

"What's that?" Jillian asked.

"Wanda Jean was in here with her new boyfriend," Maggie said. "And he's good-looking for an old guy. Plus, I saw Wanda Jean blush. I'm not kidding."

Jillian laughed out loud at that image. A widow for quite a few years, Wanda Jean had always insisted she was extremely happy being alone. *I guess romance can sneak up on any of us,* she thought. "Good for her. I hope it works out."

She snagged the pet carrier on the way out and drove over to the low building with the row of tall windows along the front. She snapped a leash on Angel and led her in, the fluffy, little dog's prancing steps making Jillian feel mildly silly somehow.

At the front desk, a heavy-set woman peered over the desk. "If you're here to complain about the leash law, we don't make the laws, we only enforce them."

Jillian looked at the woman curiously. "Do a lot of people complain about the leash law?"

The woman snorted. "Daily. You'd think letting your dogs run around and destroy other people's property was in the Constitution."

"Well, I don't have a problem with the law. I came by to chat with Deputy Zane." Just as she finished speaking, she spotted

Laura Lee weaving her way through a maze of desks. Jillian waved at her. "And there she is."

"You need to come back to my desk," Laura Lee said. "I have to fill out a report so we can be official."

"No problem. Can I bring Angel?"

The deputy smiled down at the little dog. "Sure. And is that box in your hands full of fabric scraps?"

Jillian laughed and handed the box over. "Nope, bear claws."

Laura Lee opened the lid and sniffed. "Life is good."

As they reached her desk, Jillian saw a door open nearby. Sheriff Coy Henderson strolled out, wearing the scowl that seemed to be as much a part of his uniform as the star on his chest. The sheriff was well-known for his gruff demeanor and Jillian tensed, expecting to get yelled at for bringing a dog into the sheriff's department.

To her utter shock, Angel clearly recognized the sheriff and began yapping and wagging her tail furiously. The Sheriff clumped over and scooped up the little dog to rub the underside of her chin. "I read Deputy Jones's report. He mentioned you'd taken Estelle's dog home. Thanks for that. She'll be glad to know Angel's looking so good."

That was the longest speech Jillian had ever heard from the normally laconic sheriff. She glanced sideways at Laura Lee and assumed from the deputy's gaping mouth that it was probably the longest speech she'd ever heard from him as well. Jillian cleared her throat nervously. "Well, Angel worked pretty hard to call attention to Estelle. It didn't seem right to let her end up at the pound."

The sheriff bobbed his head. "I appreciate you finding her. Estelle was my sitter when I was a little boy." He made a rumbling sound that Jillian realized was a chuckle, something else she'd never seen him do.

"Do you know how Mrs. Morgan is doing? She was unconscious when the ambulance took her away yesterday."

Again the sheriff nodded. "She's awake. I'm going over there now. I'll tell her that Angel is in good hands."

"Has she said what happened to her?"

The sheriff's eyes narrowed, making him look more like the man Jillian had met in the past. "That's sheriff's department business." Then he handed her the little dog and walked on out of the office.

Jillian and Laura Lee watched him go without speaking. Then Jillian turned to her friend. "That wasn't quite what I expected."

"Me either. Spooky." She lowered her voice to a whisper. "Though I heard his doctor said he needed to reduce his stress level for the sake of his heart. Maybe he's trying?"

"I hope it works," Jillian said. "He's kind of a grouch, but I know Bertie and Cornelia think he's an excellent sheriff."

"He is. He's smart, but he doesn't suffer fools gladly, and I think the folks who've been on his bad side are still rooting for a nice retirement party—soon."

Jillian lifted her eyebrows. "Oh, has he talked about retiring?"

"No, but hope springs eternal." Laura Lee held out a hand. "You have some fabric scraps for me?"

"Oh, yeah, right." Jillian put Angel back on the floor and pulled a plastic bag from her purse. Both scraps of fabric were inside. She dropped the bag into Laura Lee's hand, pointing as she explained which piece went with each location.

The deputy looked over both pieces. "They certainly appear to have come from the same source, probably a pair of pants. Once I fill out the report, I'll have these sent for tests, and we'll know for sure." She looked seriously at Jillian. "But it looks like whoever hurt Estelle is after you as well."

"After me?"

"Intruders at Belle Haven and a near hit-and-run certainly sound ominous to me."

Jillian felt a stir of alarm and realized she had enjoyed Gooder's dismissal of all those things better. The way Laura Lee talked made them feel real, and even more frightening.

Laura Lee pointed at her. "If you're not careful, you could be the next person shipped off to the hospital."

Jillian swallowed a sudden lump in her throat. She had the sick feeling that Laura Lee might be right.

As Jillian drove back to Belle Haven, she suddenly decided to visit Estelle. Though it was possible she'd find out what happened to the older woman eventually since the Moss Hollow gossip network was fast and thorough, she didn't want to wait or risk the distortion that came from secondhand information. At the next crossroads, she turned away from home and headed toward the Nathan County Hospital. She'd have to deal with Bertie's annoyance when she got to work much later than her grandmother expected, so she hoped the detour turned out to be worth it.

At the hospital, Jillian couldn't leave Angel in the car, but she also didn't want to lug in a pet carrier. She expected she'd be turned right around and sent back out if she tried that. She rooted in the back seat and grabbed a canvas shopping bag. "I'm taking you to visit Estelle," she told the little dog. "But you're going to have to ride in the bag."

Angel sniffed the canvas for a moment, then let Jillian tuck her into the bag. She fit with plenty of room to spare. "Try to be quiet and still, okay?" Almost as if she understood, the dog settled down in the bottom of the bag.

When she got to the reception desk, Agnes, the elderly volunteer she'd spoken with several times before was at the desk as usual, but she was joined by another older woman. Agnes recognized Jillian immediately and smiled up at her, her eyes shining. "Good morning! Who are you visiting today?" She turned to stage whisper to the other volunteer. "This is Bertie Harper's granddaughter. She visits the most interesting people here. One time it was a movie star."

Jillian smiled. "I'm here to see Estelle Morgan."

"Is *she* a movie star?" the second volunteer asked.

Agnes sighed. "No." She gave Jillian a disappointed look and then turned to the computer to find Estelle's room number. Jillian was glad Agnes didn't have a life story to share with her since she wanted to get to Estelle's room before the little dog in her bag decided to bark or wiggle.

As she navigated the confusing twists and turns to reach Estelle's room, Jillian realized she was becoming quite adept at interpreting the directions throughout the hospital. She wondered if she should consider that good or bad. To her relief, she made it all the way to Estelle's room without Angel doing anything to draw attention.

In her hurry to get inside the room with the smuggled dog, Jillian didn't pay attention to who stood at Estelle's bedside. When she saw him, she jerked to a stop.

Sheriff Henderson nodded at Jillian. "Miss Green."

At the sound of his voice, Angel popped her head over the side of the bag. Then the little dog spotted Estelle and nearly climbed right out of the bag. The sheriff walked over to help Jillian. He lifted Angel from the bag and carried her over to Estelle.

The older woman looked pale with dark circles under her eyes and a thick bandage on her head, but she smiled at the little dog and held out shaking hands. "Hello, sweetie."

Angel calmed down the instant her feet touched Estelle's bed, as if the little dog could tell her master was too delicate to handle any rowdy behavior. She lay in Estelle's lap and her little tail swept across the bedcovers. Estelle looked up at Jillian. "Thank you so much for looking after Angel. I was worried until Coy told me you had her."

"She's been enjoying watering all of Aunt Cornelia's shrubs."

Estelle laughed lightly, then winced. She raised a hand to touch her bandage lightly. "I still have a bit of a headache."

"I hope it'll remind you to be more careful and take it easy," the sheriff said. "You can't rush around like a spring chicken anymore."

Estelle huffed. "I'll follow that advice as soon as you do."

Jillian looked at Estelle in surprise. "You fell? That's how you were hurt?"

Estelle smiled tightly. "Angel rushes around my feet in the kitchen sometimes. I should know enough to be careful."

"Yes, you should." Coy leaned over to drop a kiss on the injured woman's papery cheek, then nodded at Jillian. "I'll be getting back to the office. Can't let those young deputies get used to my not being there."

"I'm sure there's not much chance of that," Estelle said.

The sheriff was chuckling as he left.

"I have to admit, I am surprised to hear you fell," Jillian said. "I found a scrap of pants fabric on the floor with Angel. I thought she tore it from an intruder." She refrained from adding the fact that the dog tore the same kind of fabric from a trespasser in the Belle Haven back garden.

Estelle's glance darted toward the door, then she waved Jillian closer. When Jillian stepped into the spot the sheriff had occupied, the older woman spoke quietly. "Is it true what folks say about you? Do you solve crimes?"

Jillian stammered a little, not sure how to answer that. "I prefer to stay away from crimes, but they do seem to thrust themselves at me."

Estelle looked her over, her expression shrewd. "I didn't fall down. I was knocked down."

"By whom?"

She shook her head slowly, but still winced again. "I didn't see the person. When I got home from church, Angel was acting oddly. She kept growling at nothing, and she was in and out the back door flap. It was frankly unnerving as she's normally a very good dog."

"I've noticed," Jillian said.

The older woman nodded. "Also, the door to my bedroom closet was ajar. Not much, but a little. I'm very meticulous about my home and I was certain I had not left the door ajar, but when I opened it, it seemed all right, except for one of my correspondence boxes."

"Correspondence boxes?"

"Yes, unlike young people today, I don't own a computer or carry around a phone that lets me talk artificially to people. When I want to correspond, I write letters and people write back. I keep every letter ever sent to me in a pair of boxes in my closet. One of the two boxes was slightly out of place."

"But you didn't see anyone?"

"No," she said. "I carried the correspondence box to the kitchen so I could make a cup of tea and go through it to see if anything was missing. I had placed the box on the kitchen counter and was on my way to the tea cupboard when someone pushed me from behind and I fell. I must have hit my head on the counter on the way down because I don't remember anything else."

"Can you describe the box?"

Estelle held out her hands to show size. "It was a pretty box. I bought it at the same craft store where I buy my crochet supplies. It was covered in floral paper with cabbage roses, and the lid was held in place with a magnet."

Jillian thought back to her discovery of the older woman in the kitchen. She tried to remember if she'd seen anything like Estelle described. She certainly didn't remember a box on the counter, but it didn't mean she hadn't seen it since her focus was on Estelle at the time.

"I would appreciate it if you'd try to find out who pushed me," Estelle said as she stroked Angel. "The doctor says I may be able to go home tomorrow, and I'm uneasy about it."

Jillian looked at the older woman quizzically. "Why did you tell Sheriff Henderson that you fell when that wasn't true?"

"It was true. I'm no liar," Estelle snapped. "I did fall and Angel does dance around my feet in the kitchen." She sighed. "Though I certainly didn't tell him that I fell because someone pushed me. I know Coy. I've known him since he was a little boy, and I was a teenager. He'll get all het up and obsessive about my having been hurt. I'm worried he'll work himself up into another heart attack. I don't want to be responsible for that."

"I'm not sure how he'll feel about my poking around in this."

Estelle waved her hand. "He's mostly bluster; don't you worry about him. You find out who hurt me, and we'll turn the person in to one of the deputies. It'll make the deputy look good and keep Coy out of trouble. Maybe he'll even believe his deputies can function without him and retire like a sensible person."

From what Jillian had heard about the sheriff, she doubted that sincerely, and she wasn't sure what Estelle was asking was a good idea, but her natural curiosity was kicking in so she asked, "Do you have any idea who would want to hurt you?"

"Hardly," Estelle said. "I'm a church organist, for heaven's sake. Why would anyone want to hurt me?"

Jillian spoke hesitantly. "I'm inclined to wonder if it may have something to do with Gracie Mae."

Estelle groaned. "Wouldn't that be perfect if that horrible woman was tormenting me from beyond the grave? But I'm certain it was human hands that pushed me, not ghostly ones."

"I expect it was too," Jillian said. "But, please, tell me more about Gracie Mae and Wallace. Why did he never file a missing person's report when she disappeared?"

"He figured she'd up and left him, and he didn't want to cause any trouble for her," Gracie Mae said. "That's how Wallace was. He didn't want to cause trouble for anyone and she took advantage of that."

"So they didn't have a good marriage at all?" Jillian said. "Not even in the beginning?"

Estelle snorted. "She punished Wallace for not being Jack Harper, plain and simple. It only got worse after Jack died. Gracie Mae had no use for Wallace at all after that. She'd hoped to make Bertie jealous, but the only emotion Bertie Harper showed over the whole mess was pity for Wallace."

"Why did he stay with Gracie Mae?"

Estelle pulled Angel closer to her, snuggling the little dog. "He loved her. He wouldn't hear a word said against her. Oh, I tried to talk sense into him, but he always believed he could get her to love him eventually. When they opened that restaurant, Wallace was sure that would be the thing that brought them together."

"But it didn't."

"Hardly. Everyone in Moss Hollow could see Gracie Mae was getting more and more disgusted with Wallace. Everything he did—catering to every demand, never sticking up for himself—made it worse. It just made it more obvious he wasn't Jack Harper."

"Did you think she left him?"

Estelle nodded. "I did. It made sense. I'd been expecting it for a while. She was secretive, even more than usual, and I thought she was getting ready to leave him. I looked forward to it, if I had to be honest. I thought it would be like cutting out a cancer. It would let my brother begin to heal, but it didn't work that way."

Estelle's comparison of Gracie Mae to cancer drew Jillian's attention sharply. At the time of Gracie Mae's death, Estelle was a younger and probably stronger woman. Jillian had certainly come into contact with murderers driven by love before. Of course, that left the question of who had knocked the organist down and who had been lurking in the garden. There were simply too many questions, and it left Jillian's head spinning.

Then Jillian remembered another important question. "Deputy Jones said they can't locate your brother."

Estelle stopped petting Angel and the little dog lapped at her fingers. "I have lost touch with Wallace. It's my own fault. My brother has suffered from dementia for the past few years. The last time I visited, he had no idea who I was. He thought Gracie Mae was in the next room. It made me cry, and my nephew got huffy with me." She sighed. "I suppose I've been petty, but if Wallace doesn't even know I'm there, and Jack can't be civil, I decided to simply let them be."

"If your brother is ill, why would they move? Wouldn't new surroundings make his life harder?" Jillian asked.

"I did get a brief letter in response to the last birthday card I sent Wallace. Jack wrote that his father was entering hospice care and would no longer be at that address. I mentioned in the card that I would come to see him this month, but in the letter Jack told me not to. He said I would be a stranger to Wallace and that strangers upset him. I haven't heard anything since. For all I know, my poor brother has passed and his son didn't tell me." She shook her head. "That boy has more of his mother in him than I'd like to say."

"If his father is so bad off, he could be overwhelmed," Jillian suggested gently.

"I suppose." Estelle's gaze dropped to her lap. "I'm feeling a little tired. Are you going to continue to look after Angel? I do appreciate it."

"Of course," Jillian said. She certainly caught the less-than-subtle hint that it was time for her to leave. "One last question, I promise. Do you know where the money came from for the restaurant?"

Estelle perked up a little at that. "That right there is the biggest mystery my family ever had. I asked Gracie Mae point blank. She told me one of her relatives had up and died, leaving her some money. But then Wallace told me the money came from him selling off his coin collection, which I knew full well wasn't worth nearly so much."

"So you believe they both lied."

"I do. One day I cornered Jack and asked him about it. He said he didn't know where the money came from, that one day his mama showed up with a sack of cash."

Jillian's mouth hung open. "A sack of cash!"

"I think Gracie Mae was a thief," Estelle said. "I scoured the newspapers for weeks, looking for news of a robbery or something like that. I never saw anything. But still, there's no legitimate way someone handed her a sack of cash. She took it from someone, and if you want to figure out who killed her, I'd say you need to figure out who she stole from. That's where your answer lies."

Whenhen Jillian pulled her car under the porte cochere on the side of Belle Haven, she sat quietly for a moment, planning her next move. She needed to get to the bakery. Already she was certain to get a first-class lecture from her grandmother about spending the morning gadding about. But she knew she wouldn't be able to concentrate on work with so many fresh questions. Gracie Mae had opened a restaurant after bringing home a mysterious bag of cash. Where had the money come from? And who might know?

From what Estelle had said, Wallace Gonce probably couldn't answer questions even if Jillian found him alive. And it sounded like Gracie Mae's son hadn't known where the money originated, at least not at the time. But he would be a grown man now, the same age as Jillian's parents. And he'd lived with his dad for years after his mom's disappearance. If anyone knew, he would. And the best way to locate Jack Gonce would be to find his dad.

"I need to find Wallace Gonce," Jillian said. She remembered that Josi had promised to try to track him down and made a mental note to call her.

Angel barked in response, jerking Jillian out of her thoughts and reminding her that the little dog might be more than ready to get out of Possum's pet carrier. "Sorry about that. Let's go in the house."

She hauled the pet carrier into the laundry room and let Angel out. The little dog danced around, clearly happy to be back in her temporary home. As Jillian hefted the carrier up onto the wall shelf where they kept it between vet visits, Possum strolled into the laundry room and exchanged sniffs with Angel.

"I have to say, I appreciate how tolerant you're being," Jillian said. The cat looked up at her with the flawlessly bored expression only a cat can manage, then turned and walked out of the room with Angel following closely behind. Jillian walked to the kitchen and poured herself a glass of sweet tea to take to her office. She hoped she could find the facility where Wallace was in hospice care. If she couldn't, she'd call Josi and hope the librarian had had better luck. Surely it was something she could manage. After all, how many hospice care facilities could Macon have?

"Jillian! What are you doing home?"

Jillian peered over her glass of tea at her great-aunt. Cornelia stood with a book in her hand that Jillian recognized as a recent purchase. It was by one of Cornelia's favorite mystery authors. "I'm dropping off Angel, and I need to look something up on the Internet."

Cornelia sniffed. "I remember a time when 'looking something up' involved the library."

"I already have Josi doing that for me," Jillian teased. "But I have Internet access here and once I get to the bakery, Bertie isn't likely to let me escape to the library."

"You took a long time at the vet's office. Is Angel all right?"

"She's fine. Dr. West said she just has a bruise. I wasn't there long. I also went to the sheriff's office, and then the hospital to visit Estelle."

Cornelia perked up. "So Estelle is awake? How is she?"

"She said the doctors told her she could possibly go home tomorrow. She also said someone shoved her and knocked her down, though she didn't see the person. That's confidential, by the way. She doesn't want it getting back to Sheriff Henderson."

"Why ever not?"

"His heart. Apparently the sheriff and Estelle are close."

"Will wonders never cease? Well, you best get on to the bakery before Bertie has an attack of her own. You know how she feels about you choosing your investigating over your duties at the bakery."

"I know. I'm only going to take a moment." Jillian hurried to her office. The click of toenails on the hard floors drew her attention to the little dog following her. "I thought you were following Possum." Angel only wagged her tail in response.

"Fine, just stay out of trouble." Jillian squeezed between the piles and taxidermy animals, making the weasel wobble and sending Angel into a frenzy of barking at him. Jillian eased into her chair, which had been made a tight fit by junk crammed behind it, keeping her from pushing it out. She turned on her laptop and drummed her fingers on the desk as she waited for it to wake up. She watched Angel fussing at the weasel. The little dog would stand on her hind legs and put her paws on the side of the tall cardboard box where the weasel was perched. That would make the weasel wobble some more, which would get the dog barking. Jillian considered putting the dog out of the office, but she didn't want to squeeze through the junk again.

She did a search on hospice care in the Macon area and was distressed to find there were a lot more options than she'd imagined in a decent-sized town like Macon. When she added in the surrounding area, she had to admit, it would take a sizable amount of time to call each one. *Time that Bertie will not appreciate.* She needed a way to thin down her choices.

"It would help if I knew where Wallace lived before," she said, mentally kicking herself for not asking Estelle. And she had to face the fact that the facilities might not give her information on their clients over the phone anyway. Medical confidentiality was an issue, as she knew. Still, she wasn't ready to give up. Then she had an idea. She actually knew one other person who definitely had Wallace Gonce's last known address, and it was even sort of on the way back to the bakery. She would go talk with Robert

Skiff, the owner of the storage company. She was fairly sure he'd give her the address.

With her plan set, she squeezed back out of the office, snagging the little dog on the way. She took Angel outside for a quick walk, put her back in the house, and then jumped into her car. "I'm on my way, Bertie," she muttered under her breath. "Just taking the long way."

To Jillian's surprise, she found Skiff had company as she walked into the office of the storage company. It was an older man with a shock of snowy white hair, a neatly trimmed beard and round wire glasses that made him look a lot like Santa Claus.

Skiff introduced them in a booming voice that suggested his guest was hard of hearing. "Hey, Lem, this is Jillian Green. She's the detective I told you about. And this is Lemuel Flagg. He used to own this place until he unloaded it on me."

Jillian gave Skiff an annoyed glance. "I'm hardly a detective. I'm Bertie Harper's granddaughter. We have The Chocolate Shoppe."

The older man hefted himself off the sofa and held out his hand. "I know Bertie right well. I remember her when she was as young as you." Then his smile widened into a grin and he turned to Skiff. "I heard this is the lady J.J. mistook for a buck. Can you imagine anyone mistaking all that wild red hair for a deer?" He burst into booming laughter at the idea.

Jillian waited for the guffaws to quiet. "I'm surprised you know about that. News sure moves fast around here."

"Well, I had a leg up. Rascal told me when I ran into him at the grocery."

"He would certainly know," Jillian said. "Though he made himself scarce right after."

The older man looked sad, lessening the Santa look. "As far as I'm concerned Rascal's been making himself scarce for years. Me and him used to be drinking buddies and sometimes hunting buddies." His sad eyes brightened. "And sometimes we were both at the same time. Look at this." He fumbled in his pocket for his wallet and pulled out a badly worn photo of three men holding rifles and grinning at the camera with arms slung around one another. He held it up. Between the creases and the fading, it was hard to identify Rascal and Lemuel, then Jillian looked more closely at the third man. He was just as unclear, but Jillian thought he resembled the man who'd bid against Cornelia for the storage unit. "Who is this?"

Flagg turned the photo back around and looked at it. "That's Rascal's little brother, Roy. He doesn't live around here anymore. I haven't seen him in years. There was a time he could keep up with Rascal and me drink for drink, and that's no small feat." He sighed. "I haven't seen Roy in years. Maybe since neither Rascal nor I drink anymore, we aren't his kind of fun. Though I don't see much of Rascal either, so maybe it's me."

"I imagine it's better for your health to give up hard drinking."

The older man laughed again. "Darlin', drinking ain't hard." Skiff joined in on the laugh. When their laughter calmed down to chuckles, Flagg spoke again. "My doctor would agree with you though. He told me I had to quit drinking or quit this earth. The jury is still out on whether it was worth it. But health didn't have nothing to do with Rascal drying up. He up and decided to quit drinking for love."

Jillian raised her eyebrows. "For love?"

Flagg chuckled again, nodding. "Rascal and I were putting away a few, well, more than a few, when back at the farm a woman wrapped her car around a tree. Rascal's wife apparently didn't appreciate that much. She almost left him not long after."

Jillian puzzled over the man's words. "You and Rascal were drinking in Atlanta?"

"Not hardly. We were up the road at the Loose Goose." He gave a dry laugh. "It ain't around anymore either. Probably couldn't turn enough profit without Rascal coming in a couple times a week to give them all his money."

Jillian wondered if her grandmother's theory had been right. Maybe there had been more than one accident involving the tree outside the Johnson farm, and now she was learning about the second one. "Do you happen to know who the woman was that hit the tree that night?"

Flagg's head bobbed, making his glasses slide down his nose. "Sure, it was that restaurant lady, the one who used to own the place with all the junk for decorations."

Jillian nodded slowly. "I know the one you mean." So Rascal Johnson had flatly lied to her. Was it because he was ashamed for not being home with his wife when the accident happened? Or was there something considerably darker behind the lie?

As Jillian was pondering the new information, her phone rang. She excused herself and stepped closer to the door to answer it. It was Maggie at the bakery. She whispered into the phone that Jillian better get there quick as Bertie was in a state over how late she was. "I'll be right there."

Between the phone call and the disquieting new information, Jillian completely forgot to ask about Wallace Gonce's old address. She left while the two men were still joking and laughing about alcohol, terrible decorating, and the mystery of making women happy. She trotted to the small parking lot near the office, as if the few seconds she was saving by running would help with Bertie's wrath when she got there.

As she drew close to her car, she froze, staring in dismay. All four tires were completely flat. More than that, she could actually see gaping holes in one of the tires. She swallowed a thick lump of fear in her throat as she looked around, wondering who had taken out so much rage on her tires and why.

16

Jillian looked around the parking lot, thinking of how exposed she must be. She quickly backed up against the office building as she raised her phone. She knew the flat tires were no coincidence and that she should force herself to go over and see if the vandal had left a note, but somehow she couldn't bring herself to move away from the false sense of security that the building gave her. With a shaky hand, she pulled out her phone and called the garage where they had all their auto work done.

In a voice she barely recognized, she described the damage to the tires and asked for someone to come out and fix them.

"Without seeing how much damage was done, I'd rather bring the car back here," the mechanic said. "I'll send a tow truck."

"I have to get to the bakery," Jillian said, distressed by how shaky and afraid she sounded.

"My cousin is here annoying me," the mechanic said and Jillian heard laughter in the background. "I'm sure he'll be happy to come give you a lift. Won't you, Paul?"

Paul must have affirmed because her mechanic assured her that he was on the way. She said she'd wait inside the storage company, and she spent the next twenty minutes being fussed over by the two men inside. Apparently she looked as scared as she felt considering how they ushered her over to the sofa and shoved a mug of coffee into her hand. She told them the bare minimum about the car, but they both had to go outside to look at it.

When they came back inside, Skiff looked at her and gave a low whistle. "Someone seems to be right mad at you."

Jillian had to agree.

When Jillian finally arrived at the bakery, Bertie had transitioned from ranting to cold fury, which was scary but quiet. Jillian threw herself into work to try to make up for being gone so much. She also hoped it would keep the questions down to a bare minimum as she wasn't feeling up to talking about the damage to the tires of her beloved Prius. She should have known better. Bertie didn't miss much.

"Why do you look so peeked?" Bertie demanded as Jillian tucked her hair into a pink hairnet. "And how come someone dropped you off outside?"

Jillian forced a weak smile and said her car had a flat. Then she amended it. "Several flats."

"I know you, young lady. Just tell me what you're trying not to tell me." So Jillian did, and her grandmother's scowl grew darker as she spoke. "I knew it. All this poking around into things is dangerous, and I don't need you doing it. Nobody was really going to think I hurt Gracie Mae Gonce, so leave it alone."

In an effort to soften her grandmother's ire and avoid admitting that she wasn't going to leave anything alone, especially after someone attacked her car, Jillian pointedly changed the subject, telling her grandmother and Lenora that she'd stopped by to see Estelle. "When I found out she was awake, I knew it would mean a lot to her to see her dog."

"And ask her a bunch of nosy questions," Bertie grumbled, still giving Jillian the stink eye with her arms folded over her chest.

Lenora looked up from where she was icing cookies. "How is she?"

"Her head still hurts," Jillian said, "but the doctor told her that she might be able to go home tomorrow."

"Good," Bertie said. "Then you can take her the dog *after* work when she gets home. I haven't had to wipe up anything yet, but where there's a dog, there's eventually a puddle."

Jillian wasn't sure if that was fair, but she knew better than to argue with Bertie in her present mood. She hefted a heavy mixing bowl into one of the smaller stand mixers to mix a fresh batch of buttercream frosting. "I'm sure Estelle will be glad to be home and to have Angel back."

"So, tell us," Lenora insisted. "Does she know who broke in?"

Jillian began scooping sugar into the large bowl. "She told Sheriff Henderson that no one broke in. She told him she fell."

"From your tone, I assume you don't believe her," Lenora said.

Bertie rested her forearms on the counter near Jillian's work area. "Of course not. Then there would be no mystery."

"Actually I don't believe her because once the sheriff left, she told me otherwise. She said when she got home from church, she saw signs of an intruder, then someone pushed her down and she struck her head. She never saw who it was." Jillian rather enjoyed Bertie's wince as she had to face the fact that Jillian had been right.

"What signs of an intruder?" Bertie asked.

"Apparently Estelle keeps all the letters she ever received in two boxes. One was out of place in the bedroom closet. When Estelle brought it out to the kitchen counter to look through it, she was knocked down."

"That's terrible," Lenora said. "Folks should have more respect for their elders."

Jillian began unwrapping blocks of butter for the recipe. "The box wasn't on the counter when I found Estelle. I'm sure I would have noticed considering how perfectly clean her house was."

"Well, if anyone can figure out what's going wrong, you can," Lenora said supportively.

Bertie stood up straight and brushed at the front of her apron. "Or else you'll keep flailing around until someone tries to kill you and gets caught that way."

Jillian wanted to say something to defend herself, but she had to face the fact that she had been in exactly that position more than once, so she simply turned her attention to the buttercream frosting and pretended the truth didn't hurt.

The rest of the workday kept Jillian so busy that she barely had time to obsess about the disjointed clues whirling around in her head. In the middle of the afternoon, someone dropped her car off in front of the bakery, and Jillian signed for it. She considered pulling it around to the back alley, which was finally available for parking again, but then decided against it. She knew Bertie didn't want anyone taking up a potential customer parking space, but Jillian wanted her car right out in the open where no one would feel safe enough to slash her tires again.

Though she stayed busy with work, Jillian couldn't help but play out her day over and over in her head. Finally she caught Lenora as she passed by with a tray of bread. "Did you ever meet Roy Johnson?"

"Rascal's little brother? Yeah. I met him. He was a wild thing. It's a wonder your mama didn't take up with him. She was always drawn to the bad boys. I expect it was probably Roy's drinking that turned her off, though, as your mama had enough of Bertie in her to disapprove of that."

"Do you know where Roy is now?" Jillian asked.

Lenora shook her head. "Haven't seen him in years, but

haven't thought much about it either. Why do you want to know?"

"I'm not sure," Jillian said. "I'm picking at loose strings, I guess."

At the end of the day, Lenora shooed both Jillian and Bertie out of the bakery. "I can lock up. I need to fuss with the sourdough starter a little before I head up."

Bertie didn't argue the point, merely reminding Lenora to put all the day old cornbread on the rack near the back door. "Someone is doing an early pickup for the senior center in the morning. They want the cornbread for stuffing."

"Isn't is a little early for Thanksgiving dinner?" Jillian asked.

Bertie shrugged. "The cook wants to have everything she needs early. At least we don't have to deliver."

The bakery had been stuck delivering to the center for months after their driver turned out to be an attempted murderer. Just the memory of that made Jillian think, once again, that Moss Hollow might be a small town but it certainly was never dull. "I'm going to run by the sheriff's office before I come home. I want to find out if Laura Lee learned anything from those fabric scraps."

"Why not call her?" Bertie asked.

"I want to tell her the truth about Estelle, but I want to be sure we're not overheard by Sheriff Henderson. Estelle doesn't want him to worry himself into a heart attack, so I need to be discreet. I've put Laura Lee in a tough spot by calling before."

"Fine, but don't lollygag. I think Cornelia is making a casserole and you know the difference between delicious and glue can be a touchy thing with a casserole. If you get home too late, I don't want to hear any complaints."

"When have I ever complained about either your cooking or Aunt Cornelia's?" Jillian asked.

Bertie began to count things off on her fingers. "Liver and onions, succotash, fried okra . . ."

"I was a teenager then," Jillian said. "Teenagers complain. That's what they do. I'm all grown up now."

Bertie's response wasn't totally intelligible as she'd turned and begun walking away, but Jillian was fairly sure she heard something about the jury being out on that. Annoyed, Jillian swept the hairnet from her head and tossed it in the trash on the way out the door. Night had fallen while she had worked in the bakery, and she took a moment to be glad of the running around she'd done during the day. It was not uncommon in the fall and winter to go a whole day without ever seeing the sun since they came in so early.

As some people were already beginning their holiday shopping, a few of the stores were adding late hours and so the drive to the sheriff's department was well lit, which helped calm Jillian's nerves. It was clear, as far as she was concerned, that someone was watching her. The intruder at Belle Haven, the near hit-and-run, and now the slashing of her tires suggested someone didn't appreciate Jillian poking at their hornet's nest, but she still had no idea which nest was producing the stings.

As she walked in the brightly lit foyer of the sheriff's office, she found Laura Lee perched on the front desk chatting with the thick-set woman in uniform who usually offered surly greetings to anyone venturing in. Laura Lee smiled at Jillian. "Did you bring more treats? The ones this morning were a big hit."

"Sorry, I'm empty-handed," Jillian said. "I'd hoped you might have something for me this time."

Laura Lee hopped off the desk, and opened her mouth, but before she could speak, Deputy Gooder Jones pushed open the front doors and strode through with a swagger that would have done well in a Western movie. "Well, as if my day couldn't get any worse, here you are."

"I didn't come to see you," Jillian replied. She turned back to address Laura Lee and discovered her friend had vanished. *Chicken!* With a sigh, she turned back to Gooder's scowling face.

"But I have no doubt that you did come to stick you nose in where it doesn't belong." He crossed his arms over his chest and smirked. "I heard that Estelle slipped and fell all on her own. That must have been quite a disappointment for you, Nancy Drew."

Jillian was tempted to tell him how wrong he was, how Estelle was pushed, but she pressed her lips together. Though she would trust Laura Lee with Estelle's secret, she wasn't nearly as sure about Gooder's discretion. Jillian settled on saying something he already knew. "That doesn't explain the piece of fabric I found at the scene."

Gooder rolled his eyes. "It was just a piece of fabric. Maybe she was doing some mending for someone. Face it, you're chasing shadows and interfering in police business. In other words, you're being the same nuisance you always are."

"Deputy Jones!"

The growl that came from the doorway leading into the bull pen made all of them freeze. Jillian saw Gooder visibly pale as he turned around to face Sheriff Henderson. "Yes, sir?"

"Tell me exactly why you're being rude to a resident of Moss Hollow, one of the citizens we are sworn to protect and serve?"

"Sir, I—"

The sheriff didn't let Gooder finish. "A citizen who has been a huge help to my dear friend Estelle Morgan." He turned his gaze to Jillian, and she fought down a flinch. "If you need something, Miss Green. I'm sure Deputy Jones will help in whatever way he can."

"Thank you," Jillian squeaked.

The sheriff passed by them all and walked out of the building. Gooder narrowed his eyes at Jillian. "What exactly do you want to know?"

"I talked to Estelle today, and she told me she felt as if there *might* have been an intruder in her house," Jillian said, thinking that might not be too far to push the confidence.

Gooder crossed his arms over her chest. "Something you probably talked her into."

Jillian raised her eyebrows. "Maybe I shouldn't bother you with this." She started to turn toward the doors. "I could still catch Sheriff Henderson."

"Fine, she believed there *might* have been an intruder," Gooder snapped. "What do you want from me?"

"I want to know if you saw any sign at all of an intruder other than the scrap of fabric I found?" Jillian asked. "Estelle kept her house obsessively neat. Did you find any open drawers or open closet doors?"

"Everyone leaves the occasional open drawer or cracked closet door."

"Apparently Estelle doesn't."

"So says you."

Jillian could see the conversation wasn't going to go anywhere useful. Since Laura Lee had deserted her, she decided she might as well go home. She made a last effort. "I think someone was in Estelle's house. Possibly the same someone who tried to run me over. And who slashed my tires today."

"Slashed your tires?" Suddenly she had Gooder's full attention. "At Belle Haven?"

"No, at the No Holds Barred Storage Company," she said. "I came out of the office and found all four tires slashed to the rims. Cost me a fortune to have them replaced."

She saw Gooder visibly relax. "Oh, actually we have vandalism over there all the time. I don't know what it is with the storage company. I couldn't tell you how many times someone has spray painted rude words on the storage-unit doors. Did you call this vandalism in?"

"No, because I knew you wouldn't take it seriously, just like you aren't taking it seriously right now. But someone is trying to scare me away from asking questions connected with Gracie Mae Gonce's death and the mysterious bag of cash she used to buy the restaurant."

"Mysterious bag of cash?" Gooder repeated.

"Estelle said Gracie Mae just showed up with a bag of cash," Jillian answered, irrationally pleased to know something he didn't. "Her nephew, Jack, told her about it."

"And she was sure the kid wasn't pulling her leg?" Gooder asked.

"She seemed sure," Jillian said, her tone tart. "About as sure as you are that there's nothing going on."

"As sure as I am that you're delusional," Gooder said. "I'll see what I can find out about the cash, and I want to remind you that we can't help you if you don't report incidents. Who did the repairs on the tires?"

Jillian gave him the name of the shop and Gooder said he'd swing by there and take a look at the damaged tires. "You do have a tendency to make folks a little crazy," Gooder said. "I think you should let this go."

"I don't think *this* is going to let me go," Jillian said, then she turned and left.

When she reached her car, she found Laura Lee standing there with her hands on her hips. "How did you like the slick way I sent Sheriff Henderson out to deal with Gooder?"

Jillian raised her eyebrows. "You did that? And I thought you deserted me."

"You might be interested to know the sheriff actually talked to me today. An actual conversation about how much help you'd been to Estelle and how every citizen ought to support their neighbors that way. I knew he'd lower the boom on Gooder if he caught him being rude to you."

"I suspect I shouldn't get used to being in the sheriff's good graces."

"Probably not," Laura Lee admitted.

Then Jillian laughed. "But it was fun seeing Gooder squirm."

"I did hear the scolding, and it's possible I recorded it on my phone to play back later," Laura Lee said, her eyes sparkling with mischief. "But you told me you needed something from me?"

"Have you gotten anything back on the cloth?"

Laura Lee gave her a puzzled look. "You're still on the cloth? Now that we know Estelle wasn't attacked, that she fell, I figured that bit of cloth wasn't relevant."

Jillian dropped her voice. "Estelle told Sheriff Henderson that she fell because she didn't want him getting worried or worked up. She was shoved, and she thought someone had been in the house. The intruder moved a box she kept correspondence in."

"That's interesting. Did Estelle tell you where she kept the box? It's possible I could get into her house and look around."

"She keeps the boxes in the closet of her bedroom, but the last time she saw it, it was on the kitchen counter. I don't remember seeing it there. I want to know if the intruder took it with him."

"I'll find out."

"Thanks," Jillian said. Then she thought of all the boxes in her office. "I'm going to go through the boxes of junk we got from the storage shed. It's possible the intruder was after some correspondence and not the map."

"Sounds like a plan. We'll get together and compare notes." Laura Lee looked back toward the sheriff's office. "I better get inside before someone sees me chatting with Gooder's public enemy number one. I'll catch you later."

Jillian hopped into her car and watched Laura Lee head into the station. What she hadn't told Laura Lee was that her plan had two steps. She was going to search the boxes, but she was also going back to the root cellar. And she knew the person she wanted along with her. She pulled her phone out of her pocket and dialed Savannah. "I'm planning a road trip in the morning. Are you up for a walk in the woods?"

"And a poke around a dark root cellar?" Savannah guessed.

"You got it."

Savannah sounded thrilled. "Of course. You know I love a good adventure."

They worked out the details and Jillian hung up, thinking of Savannah's words. She certainly hoped that this time the adventure wouldn't be quite so adventurous.

Jillian swung by the library to ask Josi about Wallace's address, but discovered the library had already closed. She'd forgotten that budget cuts had forced them into shorter hours a couple nights a week. As she pondered whether to track Josi down, her stomach growled and she decided to head home for food and search the boxes in the office.

Jillian fully intended to carry a sandwich into the office to save time as she went through the dusty boxes from the storage unit, but when she stepped into Belle Haven, the scent of fried chicken ramped up the demands from her stomach. At least part of her had no interest in getting right to work in the office.

When she walked into the kitchen, she was surprised to see a big bucket of Cheap, Cheap Chicken. She raised her eyebrows as Cornelia pulled a pan of fresh biscuits out of the oven. "Are we having a partially homemade dinner?"

Bertie stood at the stovetop stirring gravy. "I'm being practical and admitting defeat. You know that Lenora's cousin uses their family recipe for that chicken. I've never been able to reproduce it from taste and Lenora refuses to share, so the only way to have it is to buy it in a bucket."

Cornelia scooted the biscuits off into a napkin-lined basket. "That seems fair. You know, we have our family secrets too."

Bertie paid her sister no attention. "Someday I'm going to figure out what is in that coating." She pointed her slightly dripping spoon at Jillian. "Go get washed up. We're about to put it on the table."

Jillian smiled and wondered if her grandmother would always treat her as if she was still twelve, but then again Jillian knew she had been late or a no-show at the bakery more often than not recently. She recalled a favorite saying of Grandpa Jack's: "You can stay out as late as you want, but don't be late for chores." *If I want to be treated like a mature woman*, she thought, *perhaps I need to start acting like one.*

Jillian walked to the sink to wash up because there was no way she was going to miss out on that chicken. When they all sat down, they went after the food like the tired, hungry women they were, and the conversation stayed on the topic of trying to reverse engineer the Cheap, Cheap Chicken recipe until they faced empty plates and full stomachs.

Bertie took a sip from her glass of sweet tea, then sighed and turned to Jillian. "We might as well talk about what you learned at the sheriff's department."

Jillian grinned at her. "I learned all the deputies are seriously scared of the sheriff."

Cornelia snorted. "I could have told you that. Coy Henderson is a fine sheriff, but he isn't exactly cuddly."

"You should have seen him this morning fussing over Angel," Jillian said, gesturing toward the little dog that sat next to Possum, both waiting for possible chicken bits to fall to the floor. "He is apparently very close to Estelle."

"They do have a lot in common," Bertie said. "I always found Estelle to be rather brusque."

Jillian gaped at her grandmother. *Isn't that the pot calling the kettle black?* She cleared her throat to avoid saying what she was thinking and instead recounted the sheriff's dressing down of Gooder. "Honestly, I could literally see the blood drain from Gooder's face when Sheriff Henderson caught him being rude to me. I half expected him to faint."

"Poor thing," Cornelia said.

"Poor thing? Again, he was being rude to me."

"And I'm sure you were being rude to him," Cornelia said. "Honestly, I'm surprised the sheriff didn't threaten to 'stop the car' and deal with you two squabbling in the back seat."

"It would be nice if my family was on my side."

Cornelia reached across the table and patted Jillian's hand. "I'm always on your side, sweetheart. But that doesn't mean I'm blind to how you torture that young man."

"Fine," Jillian said as she hopped up from the table and picked up her plate, making Angel dance around her feet. "I guess you don't want to hear the rest, and I have work to do in my office anyway."

"And you can go do it," Bertie said, "as soon as you finish here. Your aunt and I cooked, so you clean up. You know that."

"I know." *But it certainly makes it harder to storm out of the room.* She collected the dishes as her grandmother excused herself for the night.

"I'm going to spend some time curled up in a comfy chair with a good book," Bertie said.

"Good night," Jillian called out. She carried her pile of dishes to the side of the sink in the kitchen. Her great-aunt followed behind her with a similar stack.

Jillian turned on the tap and began rinsing dishes. "You don't have to stay and help."

"I don't mind." Cornelia picked a scrap of chicken from one of the plates, tore it in half and fed it to the two eager pets.

"And that's why they hang around our feet when we try to clean up," Jillian said as she opened the dishwasher door.

"Oh, pooh, don't try to sound like your grandmother. It doesn't suit you." Cornelia pulled open a drawer and retrieved a large storage bag and began loading the leftover chicken into it. "What are you going to do this evening?"

"I'm wading through the boxes in my office. We barely peeked into some of them and there may be clues to what happened to Gracie Mae."

"That sounds reasonable. Do you want any help?"

Jillian paused, holding a dripping plate over the sink as she tried to picture squeezing her aunt into the crowded office along with her. She wasn't even certain it was healthy to breathe the air in the room crowded with old boxes and ratty, dead animals. "Thanks for the offer, but unless we drag everything out into the foyer, I don't think there's room."

Cornelia nodded. "Well, I'm going to sit in the living room and read a while. Call if you need me or if you discover anything interesting."

"I will." Jillian agreed.

Once they were done cleaning up and Jillian had wiped down the kitchen counters, she headed to her office with Possum and Angel trotting along behind her. She left the office door open, hoping the fresh air from the foyer would help ameliorate any unfortunate effects from stirring up the contents of the boxes.

Time crawled by as Jillian waded through each box. She found old receipts for food purchases for the restaurant and copies of the menu. She remembered the paper she had found in one of the menus earlier with the mysterious note: *If something bad happens remember Weasel Wednesday.* She had never figured out what the cryptic message meant. Recalling that Gracie Mae had special days at her restaurant tied to the taxidermy animals, and that one was "Weasel Wednesday," she wondered if Wednesdays were particularly bad days there.

Moving on, she found ads clipped from the newspaper and even an old news story about the restaurant opening. The clipping included a photo of Gracie Mae and her husband, both smiling for the camera. Wallace Gonce looked markedly older than his wife, and his eyes were on her instead of the camera.

With a sigh, Jillian settled into her office chair and held the picture closer to the light and examined Wallace Gonce closely. This was the man Gracie Mae had married because she couldn't get Jillian's grandfather. He had the same face shape as her grandfather and there was some resemblance around the mouth and chin, but he lacked the liveliness Jillian always remembered on her grandfather's face.

As she put the picture on her desk, her attention was drawn to a scraping sound and she looked over to see the stuffed weasel creeping slowly backward across his pile of boxes. With a shriek, Jillian jumped up and looked over the edge of the desk to see Possum pulling on the weasel's tail.

Jillian flapped a hand at the cat. "Leave that alone."

Possum paid her exactly the same attention he paid everyone who wasn't offering bacon. The weasel scooted farther across the box. Stretching as far across the desk as possible, Jillian made a grab for the weasel and managed to grab the creature's head though her grip was tenuous at best.

"Let it go," she insisted as she pulled on the weasel. She might have gotten it free from Possum, but Angel noticed the exchange and seemed to think they were playing some kind of game. She dashed over and joined in the tug-of-war, pulling on the weasel's tail even as Jillian tried to tighten her grip on the animal's head. For a moment, the struggle appeared to be a draw with neither side gaining ground. Jillian considered letting the weasel go so she could walk around the desk and shoo the pets away, but she was afraid they'd manage to drag the thing off the boxes, and the stuffed weasel was mounted on a piece of wood that might hurt them if it fell.

"Let go!" Jillian shouted, pulling as hard as she could with the grip she had. She heard Angel growling from the floor as the dog and Possum pulled back. Then suddenly Jillian's grip was more than enough and she tumbled backward with the weasel in her hands. She landed in the chair. "Got it!" *Most of it, anyway.*

Jillian realized how she'd won. The pulling had detached the weasel's tail. Jillian dropped her portion of the weasel on her desk and walked around to where the cat and dog had shifted the tug-of-war into a wrestling match for possession of the detached tail.

She reached down and grabbed the tail by the middle, then had to pry the teeth of the cat and dog—one by one—loose from the ends they held. "You two are a nuisance," she grumbled.

With the now tattered tail in one hand, she turned, determined to put the weasel where it should have been all along—the garbage bin. To her surprise, when she picked it up, she saw immediately that the threads hanging from the hole torn open during the tug-of-war didn't match the rest of the stitching on the stuffed animal. She pondered that for a moment. *It was possible*, she supposed, *the tail had come off before and someone sewed it back on.*

Holding the weasel under the light, she spotted the corner of a piece of paper crammed inside. She tried to pick the paper free but couldn't get a good enough grip on it. She walked back around the desk and settled into her chair.

"Did I hear you shouting in here?" Jillian glanced up from pulling open desk drawers to look for some tool she could use to pull out the paper. Her great-aunt stood in the doorway with a paperback book clutched in her hand.

"Possum and Angel pulled the tail off this weasel," Jillian said, "and I think someone hid something inside."

"What kind of something?" Cornelia asked, easing around a pile of boxes to get closer to the desk.

"Paper," Jillian said. "But I can't get it out."

Cornelia peered at the scrap of paper, then reached into the pocket of her skirt and held out her hand. A tatting shuttle lay in her palm. "Maybe you could use the hook at the end of this?"

Jillian thanked her as she took the shuttle and carefully coaxed the paper out. The paper turned out to be a long, thin tube and Jillian could clearly see handwriting on the paper in ink. She unrolled the sheet and found a note:

> *As I do not intend to share this with anyone, if you find this, I must be dead. And if I am dead, you should know who killed me. Recently, I was run off the road by Rascal Johnson and struck a tree, causing me severe injuries including two broken legs. Rascal Johnson was drunk at the time. I agreed to stay silent about his crime for the sake of his family. And I have no doubt I have honored that silence, but if you find this, you should know that Rascal Johnson has reason to wish me harm. If I am dead, look at him.*

The note was signed and dated nearly twenty years before. Jillian looked slowly up at her great-aunt and handed her the note. Cornelia squinted at the print and her expression darkened as she read the slip. "I can't believe this."

"But it makes some sense," Jillian said. "In fact this is the same handwriting as on a note I found in one of the menus from the Gonces' restaurant." She pulled the note from her desk. "See? 'If anything bad happens remember Weasel Wednesday.' I would never have made the connection if Possum and Angel hadn't started fighting over that stupid weasel. It looks like they are better detectives than me." Realization dawned on her. "The other thing is . . . I think we've found the source of the bag of money Gracie Mae used to open the restaurant."

"You could be right," Cornelia said. "You should call the sheriff's office. This is not something you can simply investigate on your own."

Jillian nodded as questions whirled in her head. *Is this possible? Could the secret of Gracie Mae's accident have gotten her killed? And if so, why did Rascal wait years to do the deed?*

When Jillian called the sheriff's office, she asked specifically for Laura Lee. She explained what she'd found, and Laura Lee promised to be right over. When the young deputy arrived she had Gooder Jones with her; it was all Jillian could do to refrain from groaning. She resolved to take the high road and not get into any arguments with Gooder.

She handed the note over to Laura Lee. "I was sorting through junk from the storage unit," she explained again. "Possum decided to attack the stuffed weasel. When the tail came off, I discovered this note crammed inside, under the weasel hide."

Laura Lee looked over the note and gave a low whistle before passing it to Gooder. "This is certainly interesting."

"There is more," Jillian continued. "I found this note in one of the restaurant menus." She showed Laura Lee and Gooder the note about Weasel Wednesday. "I didn't make the connection until Possum and Angel mauled the weasel."

Gooder just nodded.

"It's the same handwriting on both notes. It should be easy to prove that it is Gracie Mae's," Jillian said. "And I assume this gets Bertie off the suspect list for Gracie Mae's death. This shows Rascal Johnson had a clear motive. Gracie Mae obviously feared for her life."

Gooder took the papers from Laura Lee and frowned at them. "We'll certainly take this new information into account, but since we still don't know how Gracie Mae died, I'm not going to eliminate anything or anyone from my investigation until I get a lot more answers."

"But we'll certainly be going out to the Johnson farm to ask some questions," Laura Lee said. "So we'd appreciate it if you'd keep this between us." She included Cornelia in her look, though

Jillian's great-aunt had been uncharacteristically silent throughout the discussion so far. "We'd prefer if Mr. Johnson heard about the note from us."

"No problem," Jillian said. "I assume you'll be arresting the man. The note is pretty clear. He was driving drunk and caused an accident."

Gooder ran his fingers through his closely cropped hair. "That's complicated. We have a twenty-year-old crime with no living witness. Plus, there's a statute of limitations on crimes like drunk driving and even hit-and-runs when no one dies. This was a long time ago."

Jillian put her hands on her hips, beginning to feel frustrated. "But surely it's suspicious that Gracie Mae was run off the road by Rascal and then turns up dead on property that once belonged to the Johnsons?"

"Suspicious coincidence is a reason to investigate, but it's not enough to arrest someone," Gooder said, his brusque tone softening.

Laura Lee spoke up. "Plus, this doesn't explain your prowler. You would surely have recognized him if it was Rascal, wouldn't you?"

"Yes, but I found out Rascal has a younger brother," Jillian said. "I saw a photo. It wasn't a good photo. In fact, it was a horrible photo, but the intruder *could* have been Roy Johnson. And this note from Gracie Mae sure makes me think it might be."

"Look, we will take this seriously. And if we find enough, we'll arrest Rascal," Gooder said. "We'll do our job."

Cornelia spoke up for the first time, her tone conciliatory. "We know you will. And I will do my part here."

Gooder eyed her suspiciously. "Your part?"

Jillian's great-aunt rolled her eyes, which made Jillian stifle a giggle. "It's clear Raymond sensed the evidence in the weasel. I have to assume he is somehow in touch with the spirit of Gracie Mae Gonce."

Gooder's expression turned blank. "In touch with her spirit?"

Cornelia continued as if she hadn't heard him. "Raymond and I did eat at Gracie Mae's restaurant a time or two, but I'm surprised that's enough connection for him. I wonder if Angel could be some kind of conduit." She scooped up the little dog, who lay flopped on the floor next to Possum. She held Angel up and peered into her bugged-out eyes. "I believe I may need to have both Possum and Angel around when I use the tear-out cards." With that, Cornelia turned and left the room with the little dog in her arms and the cat trotting along behind her.

"Tear-out cards?" Laura Lee echoed.

Jillian smiled. "Aunt Cornelia uses the subscription cards from magazines to communicate with the spirit world."

Laura Lee grinned. "I'd pay good money to see that."

"Please, don't encourage her," Jillian moaned.

"Don't encourage any of them," Gooder said. "This whole household is loony."

"Goodman Jones! What would your grandmother say about your manners?"

All heads turned to see Bertie storm into the room. Even Gooder took a step back as the little woman glared at him. "Now, exactly what is going on here?"

Gooder begged off explaining everything to Bertie and practically ran out the front door with Laura Lee in tow. As she pulled the door closed behind her, Laura Lee mouthed, "I'll call you" to Jillian.

Explaining about the notes didn't take long. "Everyone knew Rascal Johnson was a hard-drinking man back then," Bertie said. "I felt sorry for Darla Johnson. She was a good woman, who deserved better than those early years with that husband. But he turned his life around and quit drinking."

"Possibly because he nearly killed someone."

Bertie nodded. "That will tend to sober a person." Her gaze turned toward the office again. "Are you done in there for the night?"

Jillian shook her head. "I expect Possum found the only real clue in all that junk, but I hate to quit until I'm really certain. Besides, it's making it easier to decide what needs to be dumped in the trash."

"Don't stay up too late," her grandmother said, then gave Jillian a kiss on the cheek and left the foyer, looking older and more tired than Jillian liked to see. *All this needs to be settled.* And with that resolve, Jillian turned back to the office to finish wading through boxes of rubbish until her nose ran from the dust and her head ached.

Jillian woke from a disturbing dream of Bertie and Gooder scolding her loudly and, at the same time, making their voices merge into a kind of roar. All the while Cornelia whispered in Jillian's ear to beware the coming of the monster. She splashed water on her face in the bathroom and tried to brace herself for confrontation. She knew Bertie would not enjoy the idea of Jillian taking more time off from the bakery, especially so close to Thanksgiving when orders were piling up.

Her prediction proved correct. Bertie carefully set down her coffee mug to focus her death glare on Jillian. "You did come all the way back to Georgia to help with the bakery, right?"

"Actually I came back because I lost my job, my fiancé, and my self-respect all in the same week," Jillian said. "You'd been trying to make me feel guilty about the bakery for years before that."

Bertie's glare never let up. "You got sassy out in California."

"Don't be silly," Cornelia scolded her sister as she surreptitiously tossed bits of bacon to Possum and Angel. "Jillian has been sassy all her life. All the Belle Haven women are sassy."

Bertie pointed at her sister. "Stop encouraging her. And stop feeding the animals at the table."

Cornelia sniffed. "You are not the boss of me, Bertie Harper. Possum and Angel worked very hard last night. First, they brought an important clue to Jillian. Then they helped me. I believe they really empowered the tear-out cards."

Bertie gave her sister a withering look. "If I ask nicely will you, please, not tell us about the tear-out cards anymore?"

Cornelia ignored her. "With the help of Raymond and whomever Angel is connecting with . . ." She turned to smile down at the little dog. "I'm still not sure who that is. But, at any rate, when I laid out the cards I got a cooking magazine with bagels on the cover, a children's magazine with Smokey the Bear on it, and a card from a mystery magazine."

Jillian stared at her aunt. "And that meant?"

"It couldn't be more obvious," Cornelia said. She looked from Jillian to Bertie and back to Jillian. "You two really can't see it? The spirits are saying that as you investigate the mystery you must beware the bagel, or maybe beware the hole or the bakery. These things can be a little ambiguous."

"Beware the hole?" Bertie said. "Where did you get that?"

"The bagels, of course." When Bertie continued to look at her blankly, she added. "They have a hole in the middle."

As much as Jillian appreciated her great-aunt's distraction, she did worry sometimes about Cornelia's mental acuity. If Cornelia didn't prove herself so sharp in other areas, Jillian might be inclined to haul her off to a doctor. *She's eccentric, not crazy.* "Well, I am going back to the root cellar. That is a kind of hole, I guess."

"See," Cornelia crowed. "So you be sure to be careful out there today." She narrowed her eyes. "You're not going alone, are you?"

Jillian shook her head. "No, Savannah is coming over and we're going together."

"Good," Bertie said. "She's a little too easily led astray by you, but otherwise, that girl's got a good head on her shoulders."

Jillian didn't appreciate being painted as the bad influence, but she was happy Bertie was showing signs of accepting her trip out to the root cellar. "I promise this is the last morning I'll miss this week."

Bertie snorted. "Don't make promises you can't keep. I know I've taught you that much. You and Savannah run off on your investigation. Lenora and I can handle things this morning, but I really do need all hands on deck if we're going to keep up with orders. We've been taking on more now that you can be trusted with the ovens."

"I certainly plan on this being my last morning off," Jillian said. *That, at least, was completely true.*

When Savannah arrived, she carried a backpack hung on one shoulder. "I brought this since I didn't know if you wanted to take your car or mine."

"We'll take mine," Jillian said. "It's got brand-new tires."

"I heard about that," Savannah said. "How horrible that must have been. I would completely freak out if someone slashed the tires on my car. I don't even let it get dirty for very long."

"I thought you were the outdoorswoman," Jillian said.

"I am," Savannah insisted. "I just clean up afterward." She hefted the bag higher on her shoulder.

"What do you have in that thing?" Jillian asked. "We're poking around the root cellar a little, not camping."

"I'm well aware of the plan for the morning," Savannah said. "And you'll be glad when you get hungry or thirsty while we're out there and I have snacks."

"I can't argue with that."

As they drove out toward the Johnson farm, Jillian caught Savannah up on the note she'd found in the weasel and her encounter with Gooder Jones. "You could try to look on the bright side," Savannah said. "You don't work with him. Poor Laura Lee."

"I don't know. About half the time, I think she finds him amusing."

Savannah shifted in her seat, adjusting the seat belt at her shoulder. "I sometimes wonder if there is a perfect height for wearing seat belts where they don't try to saw into your skin, and everyone else gets to suffer."

"If there was," Jillian said. "They'd make a documentary about him, the perfect seat belt guy."

Savannah chuckled and threw ideas out about the seat belt

guy documentary until they were both laughing. From there, they started trading funny work stories. From the sound of it, Savannah had worked on the books for half the people in Georgia, though Jillian had some great stories from her time working at the ad agency in California. "And then one of the assistants looked at me wide-eyed and said, 'People actually eat the skin off a pig?'"

When the laughing finally subsided, Savannah pointed up ahead. "We're nearly at the Johnson farm."

"Let me know if you see sheriffs' cars," Jillian said. "I have to keep my eyes on the road on this curve. I can understand how easy it was for Rascal to run Gracie Mae off the road. That curve is tricky in the daylight and cold sober."

"That must have been terrifying for her," Savannah said, her gaze intent on the road ahead, clearly watching for the first glimpse of the farm. Jillian completed the turn and Savannah called out. "I saw a sheriff's department car, but I didn't see any people."

"They could have gone inside to talk," Jillian said. "Gooder doesn't enjoy standing out in the cold."

Savannah looked over at Jillian. "I have to admit, I'm really enjoying the cooler weather, I thought I would roast to death this summer."

"Roast or melt," Jillian said. "You should try hanging out in the kitchen at the bakery."

"I think I'll pass." Savannah crossed her arms over her chest. "Do you really think Rascal killed Gracie Mae?"

"I don't know," Jillian said. "Though I suspect he's the reason she was in that root cellar. Clearly Gracie Mae knew something that Rascal wouldn't want spread around. And I wonder if Rascal might have been the source of the money Gracie Mae used to open her restaurant."

Savannah gave Jillian a quick glance, her brow furrowed. "Where would Rascal get that kind of money? He's a farmer."

"I didn't say I knew." Jillian drummed a finger nervously on the steering wheel. "But apparently he sold off some land around then. The story was that he did it to pay off taxes, but maybe he did it to pay off Gracie Mae. And it's possible that Rascal wasn't the only person she blackmailed."

"You talk as if her blackmailing Rascal was a sure thing."

"Her note flatly said she was worried about Rascal hurting her," Jillian said, "which says to me that she'd done something besides assuring him she wouldn't blame him for her wreck."

At that, they turned another corner and reached the pull-off they'd used on the day of the ill-fated treasure hunt. Jillian pulled off the road and Savannah grabbed her backpack, grunting from the weight.

"Do you want me to carry some of that stuff?" Jillian asked. "I think I have a bag in the trunk that we could switch some to."

"Nope, I'm good," Savannah said. "It's not heavy if you carry it right."

Right. Jillian walked to the back of the car and froze. "We don't have the bright orange vests that we wore last time. Those belonged to Laura Lee. We could seriously get shot out there."

"As I said, I'm prepared." Savannah shifted the bag off her back and onto the trunk lid of the car. She pulled out a bright orange scarf printed with tiny black cats and handed it to Jillian. "This should work."

As Savannah delved back into the bag, Jillian wrapped the scarf around her neck, leaving plenty of it dangling. Savannah pulled out a length of bright orange fabric, which she folded and wrapped like a scarf around her own neck.

"So dare I ask where this came from?" Jillian asked. "Blaze orange isn't one of your usual color choices."

"I bought it for a costume I planned to make for Moss Holloween, but I didn't end up using it. James and I came up with costumes together." She tossed the frayed end of the fabric around her neck with a flourish. "But it came in handy after all."

And I barely feel silly at all, Jillian thought, but she didn't want to hurt her friend's feelings so she simply agreed, and then waited for Savannah to slip the backpack on her shoulders and lead the way into the woods. The quiet in the woods seemed even more profound, and Jillian was glad to find they didn't hear a single gunshot as they stomped through the woods to the root cellar. Savannah used the GPS on her phone to guide them, and the trip seemed to take considerably less time. When they reached the creek and turned toward the root cellar, Savannah pointed at the cloth Laura Lee had tied to a bramble to mark the spot where the sinkhole opened into the cave below. "Without that, I would never have seen that spot," Savannah said. "And one of us could have ended up back in it."

"Which I certainly wouldn't enjoy."

They made their way through the overgrown foundation area, the previous damage they'd done to the brush when they stomped through the first time seemed to have mostly vanished and Jillian marveled at how quickly nature covered up the signs of human passage through wild places.

When they got to the cellar door, Savannah shucked off the backpack again and rooted through the contents until she found two flashlights. She handed one to Jillian. "This should help us look around in there." Jillian couldn't help but notice the "I came prepared" smile on her friend's face, but she figured Savannah deserved a chance to be smug since Jillian hadn't thought to bring a flashlight, even though she'd already been inside the dark, dank cellar.

The inside of the cellar still smelled strongly of damp soil and must, but there seemed to be some smell missing, and Jillian assumed it must have been the smell of very old bones. Even with the skeleton gone, Jillian could have drawn the exact spot on the hard packed dirt. The image was burned into her memory.

Jillian had planned for the need to crawl around on the ground by wearing old worn jeans. "I'll search low and you check out the shelves."

"Sounds good."

After a slow, careful search Jillian found the carcass of a dead mouse, a surprising number of old dry leaves, and enough cobwebs to equip a haunted house. What she didn't find were any clues. "Nothing here," she said, sitting back on her heels. "How about you?"

"I discovered okra doesn't look any more appealing after it's been in a jar for a decade or two," Savannah said. "And I found some really tiny bones. I think they might be from a bird."

"This is a fun spot," Jillian said sarcastically as she stood up and brushed the dirt from her knees. "We might as well get out of here."

The shadowy clearing seemed blindingly bright after stepping out of the dark cellar. Jillian walked over to sit on one of the intact parts of the old stone foundation. "I was sure we'd find something helpful here."

"Well, it makes sense that we didn't," Savannah said, though her own disappointment colored her voice. "The deputies would have done a really thorough search themselves."

"I feel that we're really close to the answer. It's as if it's right in front of me but I can't quite reach it." She reached out to the empty air, then dropped her hand back into her lap. "Who knows? Maybe Rascal confessed and it's actually all over. Maybe we're just out here for a walk in the woods."

"Could be," Savannah said agreeably. "But if it wasn't Rascal, who else would possibly have been angry enough at Gracie Mae? I know Gracie Mae put a lot of effort into annoying Bertie. Are we sure Bertie's the only person she ever targeted?"

"Honestly, I don't know much. I know Estelle disliked, and maybe even hated, Gracie Mae because of how she treated Wallace."

Savannah wrinkled her nose. "I have trouble visualizing Estelle as a killer."

"I agree, plus someone broke into her home and tried to hurt her." Then Jillian put her hand to her mouth. She'd not actually intended to share that news.

Savannah, of course, jumped right on it. "I heard she said she fell."

Jillian came clean about what Estelle had said in the hospital. "Please don't tell anyone. I've already proven to be the worst person on the planet at secrets."

Savannah laughed. "Secrets aren't easy to keep in Moss Hollow."

"No, they're not." She looked at her friend. "You know, I wonder if that is what motivated Wallace's move to Macon. A man with a secret would need to move away to keep it."

"Wallace Gonce?" Savannah laughed at that. "I know you were gone so you never met him, but that man wouldn't say 'boo' to a mouse. He was definitely no killer."

"Still, living with someone who makes you miserable is tough. Maybe he snapped."

Savannah still looked dubious. "You wouldn't say things like that about him if you'd ever met him."

"Maybe that's what I need to do next," Jillian said. "Maybe I need to make a road trip to Macon and talk with Wallace Gonce. He's the only other person who may have some insight into his wife's death."

"Do you know where he lives?" Savannah asked. "I thought that was an issue."

"Estelle said Wallace is in hospice care. I found a list of the facilities that offer hospice care in that area, I can try carrying a bouquet of flowers into each of them and saying I'm there to visit Wallace Gonce."

"If he's in hospice, what makes you think he'll be well enough to talk about Gracie Mae?"

"I don't know," Jillian said. "I need to do something." At that, she leaned forward sharply to put her head in her hands, more as a dramatic gesture than anything. But the moment she dipped forward, she heard the bark and whine of a bullet fired close by. The bullet hit the pile of stones behind the spot her head had been only moments before.

Someone was trying to kill her!

"Stop shooting!" Jillian yelled, throwing herself to the ground beside Savannah, "There are people over here." Savannah joined in the shouting until another bullet struck the wall. With all the yelling, there was no way someone thought they were deer.

"Someone's trying to kill us," Savannah whispered frantically.

Jillian looked around, hoping to find a more secure spot for them to hide. She gestured along the wall where the ground dipped, giving them more protection. "That way." She began to crawl toward the lower ground with Savannah right beside her.

Just as they reached the spot, another bullet struck the wall where they'd crouched earlier. Clearly the shooter thought they were still there.

"Why do people keep shooting at me?" Jillian whispered.

"How long do you think it'll be until whoever that is figures out he can just walk over here and shoot us since we're not armed?"

"Hush. We don't want to give him any ideas." Jillian pulled her phone from her pocket. The screen was cracked from her dive and crawl across the ground, but she had a signal and quickly dialed Laura Lee. Her friend answered on the first ring. "I'm out at the root cellar with Savannah. I think Rascal Johnson is shooting at us."

"Not likely," Laura Lee said. "Since I'm looking at him."

"In that case, it's probably Rascal's brother Roy. I'm not so worried about identification at the moment. I'm more focused on survival."

"Are you sure it's not another deer hunter?" Laura Lee asked. "Have you tried calling out?"

"Yes," Jillian whispered fiercely. "And he used it to zero in on our position and shoot some more. We'd appreciate some help here."

"We're on our way. Keep your heads down."

As soon as Jillian ended the call, she turned to Savannah. "I'm not sure how fast Laura Lee can get here. We're going to have to do something before we get shot."

"What?" Savannah asked. "Shoot back with our nonexistent gun?"

Jillian's eyes widened. "Yeah." She pulled out her phone and connected to the Internet."

Savannah leaned over her shoulder. "What are you doing? Looking for tips on escaping from gunmen?"

Jillian shook her head and cranked up the volume on her phone. "No, I found us a gun." She handed the phone to Savannah. "Stay low, but play this sound file. If the shooter believes it, it might distract him enough for me to get behind him."

"Are you crazy?" Savannah whispered. "You want to get killed?"

"Of course not, but I also don't want to wait here for him to walk up and shoot us point-blank." She pointed at Savannah. "Stay here. Stay low. Play the sound."

Savannah began talking loudly about the gun in the bottom of her purse, and how she thought she could reach it. A shot rang out, knocking some bits from the rock wall behind where they were hidden. Then Savannah yelled. "Got it!" And she pressed the button on the phone. The gunshot rang out and Jillian was surprised at how chillingly real it sounded. She gave Savannah a thumbs-up and began crawling away.

Savannah kept talking loud, and pushing the button now and then. The shooter fired back once in a while, knocking more pieces from the rock wall. Jillian crawled faster and made it to the tree line at the end of the crumbling foundation wall. She stayed low and followed the sound of the shots from the woods.

Ahead she spotted a swatch of gray. She was finally close.

She picked up a heavy stick and crept toward the gray as quietly as possible. From what she could tell, the shooter was standing as still as a statue. *He's probably hoping to catch Savannah peering over the wall.* She certainly hoped she could whack the guy in the head before he managed to do just that. She dodged around a thick tree and froze. She finally had an unobstructed view of what she'd thought was the shooter. Instead, she was looking at a gray jacket hooked on a thick tree branch. At the same moment, she froze as she felt something hard jab her in the middle of the back.

"Thanks for making this easy," a low voice said behind her. "You go ahead and turn around, Miss Green."

Jillian turned slowly with her hands in the air. She faced the man who had bid against Cornelia in the auction and tried to break into Belle Haven. "Roy Johnson?" she said.

The man frowned. "What?"

"I know who you are," she said. "You're Roy Johnson."

He laughed. "Hardly. You really don't have a clue, do you?"

She swallowed the lump in her throat. "Jack Gonce."

He smiled. It wasn't a pleasant look on him. "That's right. Only took two guesses."

"Why did you kill your mom?" she asked.

The smile vanished and he glared at her. "I did not kill my mother. I didn't mourn her much, but I didn't kill her."

"Then what are we doing here?" she demanded. "And why did you attack your aunt?"

"I didn't," he insisted. "Or, I didn't want to. I wanted some of the letters my dad wrote. I knew she kept all the letters she'd ever gotten and I had to be sure he never said anything incriminating. I didn't want her to see me. I thought I could knock her down and get away before she could get up and see me. I didn't intend to actually hurt her."

Jillian looked pointedly at the gun. "The way you don't intend to actually hurt me?"

The barrel had been trembling slightly with his emotion, but now it grew steady as he smiled and said, "No, I fully intend to hurt you."

"Why? What is behind all this? If you didn't kill your mother, who did?" Jillian asked.

His lips tightened grimly and for a moment Jillian thought he was going to shoot her instead of answering her question, but finally he spoke. "My father did. He thought she was cheating on him. It wouldn't have been much of a surprise. It was certainly clear to me that Mom despised Dad."

"Cheating with whom?"

"Dad followed Mom out to the old homestead over there." He gestured quickly with the gun barrel before bringing it back to bear on Jillian. "Mom met with Rascal Johnson, but Dad saw right away that it wasn't romantic."

"She was blackmailing him."

The gunman nodded. "She wanted him to pay her more money for keeping quiet about his drunk driving. Apparently he'd done it before."

"Which is how she got the money for the restaurant."

He nodded again. "But Johnson refused to pay. In fact, he said a lawyer told him the statute of limitations on his crime was up years before, so she could forget about getting another thin dime from him. In fact, he said he was considering suing her to get back the money he'd 'loaned' her to open the restaurant. Mom apparently was furious about it and attacked the guy. She managed to scratch his face before he knocked her down. I know it's been a long time, but I bet they're going to find DNA evidence against Johnson when all the tests come back. That should keep the cops following the wrong trail and keep my dad safe."

"I still don't understand why your father killed her."

"Apparently when Rascal knocked her down, she screamed that she would get the money from him somehow. She'd tell people he attacked her. Anything to get enough money to get out of town and away from my father. Apparently she said some pretty horrible things about my dad."

"And your dad loved her," Jillian said softly.

"He did." The gunman's face tightened in anger. "It made no sense. She was horrible, but he loved her. And when he heard her say those things about him and about their marriage, he snapped. He said he waited until Rascal stormed out, then he went into the root cellar, grabbed her and yelled at her and when he was done, she wasn't breathing anymore."

"He strangled her."

"He doesn't remember doing that, but yeah, he must have. But my dad isn't like that. She put him through years of the worst kind of verbal abuse, but hearing her say it to someone else was apparently too much."

"So you and your dad ran."

He nodded. "I had to handle everything. Dad wasn't much more than a zombie. He would have turned himself in. I couldn't let him spend the rest of his life in jail for her. He'd already suffered enough. So I put the restaurant stuff in storage and moved us to Macon. Dad got better over time and we were doing well until he got so sick."

"And you stopped paying for the storage unit."

"I didn't think we needed it. We didn't want that junk, and we weren't coming back here. Dad's medical expenses were so high." He shook his head and again the barrel wavered. Jillian tensed, wondering in the moment if she dared try to grab the gun, but he shook off the distress and the gun steadied on her again. "Then I was visiting Dad at the hospice and he told me about that stupid map. He wanted to make sure someone found mom eventually. He'd drawn it on some old animal skin Mom had. Dad hid it in the storage unit back when he wanted to be caught and punished."

"So you came to Moss Hollow to get it back."

"And I would have, if you hadn't been so nosy. You never quit. Even with the sheriff out at the Johnson farm, you had to keep picking away. You were never going to let it go, and I can't have them looking for my dad. He might confess everything, and I won't have my dad spend his last few months in prison."

"Killing me isn't going to keep you safe."

"Maybe not. But it'll definitely keep me safer." He raised the gun high, sighting down the barrel and Jillian knew there wouldn't be any more discussion. He was going to kill her.

20

"No one is going to believe Johnson killed me," Jillian insisted. "Not with the deputies at his house."

The gun barrel didn't waver. "No, but he gave me the idea for what they will believe. Folks get killed out here wandering in the woods without proper gear in deer hunting season."

Jillian shook her head. "That won't work. I called for help when the shooting started. The deputies are on their way here."

He smiled. "Sure they are. Nice try though." He gestured back toward the foundation. "But now that I think about it. It might be better if something else happened to you and your friend. Maybe you were stomping around and you fell off into the river. It's quite a drop. Let's go get her."

Jillian definitely didn't want to lead Jack Gonce back to Savannah. "You don't want to go back there. Savannah's got a gun."

"Yeah, I know all about that. That was clever. You fooled me at first, but no one can shoot that many times and not hit anything, not even a tree. I figured out it wasn't a real gun from listening." He gestured with the barrel of the gun and, since Jillian couldn't see any choice, she walked ahead of him toward the old foundation. As she walked, she murmured a quiet prayer for Savannah's safety and hers.

"What?" Jack demanded, poking Jillian in the back with the end of the barrel.

Jillian jumped. Either he had very sharp ears or she was praying louder than she thought. "I was praying."

"Good idea," Jack said.

When she stumbled into the clearing, she was relieved to see no sign of Savannah. "Come on out," he demanded.

Nothing moved.

"I'm not playing, lady," he shouted. "If I don't see you in the count of ten, I'm going to shoot your friend." He started counting.

Don't come out, Jillian thought, trying to show the words on her face. *If he is going to shoot me, then good enough. But at least Savannah will survive.* She was only out there because Jillian had suggested it.

Jack made it all the way to eight before Savannah cracked and stepped out from behind a tree at the opposite edge of the clearing. She had her hands in the air. "I'm here. Don't shoot Jillian."

"Good move. You didn't want to watch your friend get shot. It's better to go out together." He gestured with the gun barrel again. "Miss Green, walk over there with your friend, and we'll head for the river."

Jillian exchanged miserable expressions with Savannah, lagging until Jack poked her again with the barrel of the gun. She started toward Savannah. Then she felt a rush of hope when she spotted the blue bandanna and realized the most direct path across the clearing would take them right over the sinkhole. She knew Jack had been around the day they found it, but had he been there from the very beginning? Did he know about the hole? Subtly, she began to edge toward it as she stumbled along as clumsily as possible.

"Pick up your feet," Jack demanded. "It's a wonder you've survived as long as you have."

"My grandmother tells me that all the time," Jillian grumbled, using another stumble to take them still closer to the hole. If he wasn't aware of the hole, all she had to do was get past it while still leading him into it.

Savannah must have caught on to what Jillian had in mind

because she began walking away from the tree line, bringing the space between them still more in line with the sinkhole. "Hold it right there," Jack shouted at her. "Just stand still. I appreciate your eagerness but we'll get to you."

Hopefully, only one of us will, Jillian thought frantically as she intentionally stumbled and fell, lining them up with the sinkhole better. Jack growled at her as she scrambled back to her feet. "Give me a break," she snapped. "I'm not really the wilderness type."

"You should have remembered that before you came back out here to stick your nose where it didn't belong."

Jillian didn't dare look back at him to make sure his attention was on her and not the ground. She needed to keep him occupied. It was only a few more yards. "You in a hurry?" she asked.

"Actually I am," he said. "Whatever you might think, killing you isn't the highlight of my day. It's just something that has to be done."

"It doesn't," Savannah said. "You could leave us here and run."

"Or I can kill you and never have to run again," he replied.

Jillian suddenly thought of a question. "How did you know we were out here, anyway? Have you been watching Belle Haven all this time?"

"I didn't have to," he said with a bark of laughter. "My new girlfriend told me. She is seriously plugged into the gossip at Belle Haven, especially anything connected to you."

"Your girlfriend?" Then in a flash, Jillian knew who he was talking about. "Wanda Jean. You brought her to the bakery! How did you know I wouldn't see you and recognize you?"

"I didn't, but she was determined to get me to taste a Chocolate Shoppe bear claw. The risk was actually kind of exhilarating."

Poor Wanda Jean, Jillian thought. After this she'd *really* never want to consider dating again.

"The sheriff's department will track you down," Savannah

shouted at Jack, drawing Jillian's attention back to her plan. "Our friend Laura Lee will never let it go."

As Jack laughed at Savannah's faith in her friend. Jillian realized that Savannah was intentionally drawing his attention, making it easier for Jillian to move toward the sinkhole, so she stayed as quiet as possible as she watched the ground ahead of her for the edges of it. If she got too close, she might fall in herself, especially if the ground crumbled away. If she was too far, she stood the chance of Jack not falling in.

Finally she was as close to the hole as she dared get. She pretended to stumble and threw herself across the end of the hole. As soon as she hit the other side, she scrambled across the ground toward a pile of rocks.

"Hold it!" Jack shouted behind her. "I'll shoot. Hold it."

Then several things happened so closely together that to Jillian they seemed to be all one event. Jack crashed toward her, then yelled in shock and surprise, signaling his fall into the sinkhole. As he fell, the gun went off. And fire seemed to rip past Jillian's hip. *I've been shot!*

Despite the sounds of his falling and the pain in her hip, Jillian didn't stop scrambling across the ground until she was behind a crumbling section of foundation wall. Savannah joined her there in moments. They could hear scrabbling sounds from the sinkhole as Jack tried to climb out. Jillian just hoped he wouldn't be successful.

"You're bleeding," Savannah said.

"I noticed." Jillian moaned as she shifted her weight. Her hip burned viciously and her dark jeans were growing darker with the stain of blood. "If Gooder shows up, let me know." She unfastened her pants and looked in. Her hip had a nasty gash, but she managed a weak grin. "It's only a flesh wound. Do you have any bandages?"

Savannah nodded and shucked off her backpack. She produced a thick roll of gauze which Jillian stuffed into her pants over the gash. "That should help. I think I can walk."

"Normally I'd say you should lay still until help comes," Savannah said.

"This is not normal, and I'd just as soon get as far from Jack as possible," Jillian said. "He may be a better climber than Laura Lee." Though from the sounds they heard coming out of the hole, it didn't sound like he was. Savannah helped Jillian to her feet.

They started across the clearing with Jillian quickly discovering that there was no point in limping as every movement of her body seemed to make the burning pain worse. She gritted her teeth and walked as steadily as she could. They'd gotten about halfway across the clearing away from the sinkhole when they heard rustling in the brush beyond and Gooder Jones burst out of the woods with Laura Lee right behind him.

"We heard a gunshot," Laura Lee said.

"And I felt it," Jillian quipped, though even she could hear the strain in her voice. She turned toward the sinkhole, wincing at a fresh rush of pain and pointed. "You'll find Estelle's attacker in the sink hole. It's Jack Gonce."

"He was going to kill us!" Savannah added.

"Be careful," Jillian added. "He has a rifle."

Gooder demanded Jack throw out the gun. Since he didn't have much choice, he complied. Laura Lee helped Savannah settle Jillian on a rock so she could look at her wound. Savannah took up a position blocking Gooder's view, though Jillian suspected the deputy had enough on his plate getting Jack out of the hole.

"I think the bullet only grazed you," Laura Lee said. "The main thing we have to worry about is infection."

"Savannah probably has antibiotics in that bag of hers," Jillian said, panting slightly from the pain of Laura Lee poking around her wound. "She might even have a doctor."

Jillian was rather proud of the fact that she didn't cry or whimper—much—as Laura Lee finished bandaging her wound properly.

"That should do until we can get you to a hospital," she said.

Jillian shook her head. "I don't need a hospital. I'll swing by the clinic before I go to the bakery."

"The bakery!" Savannah echoed. "You cannot be planning to work. You got shot."

"Grazed." Jillian winced as she hauled herself to her feet. "Bertie is not going to consider that a reason to miss work. She has a kind of pioneer stock thing going. Anything short of limb loss should just be toughed out. So, do I have to stay to swear out a complaint about being shot or can I leave?"

Laura Lee pulled out a notebook. "Go over everything that happened. Then you can leave."

So Jillian settled back down painfully and began.

Jillian quickly discovered driving was an issue with her hip feeling as if a ball of fire was slowly chewing its way into her, so she handed over the keys to her Prius and settled into the passenger seat as comfortably as she was able. Savannah drove her to the clinic and waited as Jillian found out she actually could be in more pain than she'd already felt. But in the end, the doctor gave her a prescription for some pain medication that sounded like it might be the highlight of her day. Savannah flatly refused to take her to the bakery and since they had to go to Belle Haven for Savannah to pick up her car anyway, Jillian gave in. She was pretty sure she could talk Cornelia into driving her to work.

To her surprise, she found both Bertie and Cornelia waiting for her at the house. As they fussed over her, Jillian turned to her grandmother. "What are you doing home from work?"

"My granddaughter was shot," Bertie snapped. "Where else would I be?"

"How did you know I was shot?" Jillian shot a glance at Savannah and saw guilt all over here face. "You ratted me out?"

"Don't you yell at her," Bertie said. "Besides, Laura Lee called me as well. Now, we need to get you upstairs to bed."

"Bye, Jillian," Savannah sang out as she backed out the front door. Jillian scowled after her. *Chicken.*

"I thought I'd go to the bakery," Jillian said, though bed sounded fantastic.

"Stop being silly." Bertie turned to her sister. "Can you get Jillian something to eat? She shouldn't take pain medication on an empty stomach."

"I'll be glad to." Cornelia turned and hurried away with Possum and Angel at her heels displaying an eagerness that suggested they'd guessed she was on her way to the kitchen.

Jillian started the slow painful walk up the stairs, leaning heavily on the railing with Bertie right beside her watching every movement like a hawk. "Sorry about not coming in to the bakery."

"Don't be silly," Bertie said. "We'll manage. By the way, Josi came by the bakery. She brought Wallace Gonce's address at a hospice care facility."

"Gooder will appreciate having that. Though I kind of hope they let the poor man die in peace." Jillian spoke through gritted teeth, trying not to pant from the pain as they made it up the next step. "You're taking this well."

"How else would I take it?" Bertie scooted under Jillian's arm to add a little lift with each step. "That's just the way the cookie crumbles."

"You've been a little grumpy lately," Jillian said. She held up a hand. "Give me a second. I need to rest."

Bertie nodded. "I know I've been a little short. All of this has stirred up a lot of feelings about your grandfather. I miss him terribly. You know, we fought once or twice about Gracie Mae. He thought I could have been kinder to her. And I thought she deserved a punch in the face."

"As it turns out," Jillian said, leaning heavily on the rail, "you were right."

That made her grandmother smile. "He was right too. I let that silly feud steal moments away. That's the thing I guess I wish I could undo. I want to gather up all the moments that were wasted or taken for granted and I want a chance to redo them. That would be glorious."

"I wish you could have that," Jillian said. "But Grandpa Jack knew you loved him. It was all over both your faces so often."

"Thanks," Bertie said. "Maybe you'll have that someday too."

Jillian rolled her eyes as she braced herself for the next step. "Sure. Since my love life is going so well."

"It would if you'd give Hunter more of your time and attention," Bertie scolded as Jillian hauled herself up the next step. "He's clearly smitten with you and you waste time gallivanting around Moss Hollow chasing after things better left to the police."

"If you'll remember," Jillian panted. "I saved you from being arrested."

"Pishposh," Bertie said. "Gooder Jones wouldn't have dared."

Jillian had to give her grandmother that one. It was possible he wouldn't have. As she hauled herself up the next step, she realized that despite the pain in her hip, things could finally go back to normal—or what passed for normal in Moss Hollow.

And to her surprise, she found she liked that idea just fine.

The Cookie Crumbles
Book Seven Recipe

Pumpkin Spice Cookies

2½ cups all-purpose flour
1 teaspoon baking powder
1 teaspoon baking soda
1 tablespoon pumpkin pie spice
½ teaspoon salt
1 cup white sugar

½ cup dark brown sugar
½ cup softened butter
1 cup canned pumpkin
2 eggs
1 teaspoon vanilla

Instructions

Preheat oven to 350 degrees.

1. Combine flour, baking soda, baking powder, pumpkin pie spice, and salt in medium bowl and set aside.

2. Beat both sugars, butter, and eggs in a large bowl until thoroughly blended. Add pumpkin and vanilla and beat until smooth. Beat in flour mixture, adding in ½ cup increments.

3. Drop cookies on greased cookie sheet in one tablespoon amounts. Using damp finger, flatten each cookie slightly.

4. Bake 15 to 18 minutes. Cool for three minutes, then move to wire rack to finish cooling.

Cookies can be iced, dusted with powdered sugar, or made into whoopee pies with a cream-cheese frosting.

Learn more about Annie's fiction books at

AnniesFiction.com

- Access your e-books
- Discover exciting new series
- Read sample chapters
- Watch video book trailers
- Share your feedback

We've designed the Annie's Fiction website especially for you!

Plus, manage your account online!

- Check your account status
- Make payments online
- Update your address

ANNIE'S ATTIC
MYSTERIES®

CREATIVE WOMAN
MYSTERIES®

Annie's
Quilted
Mysteries™

Annie's
Mysteries
Unraveled™

AMISH
INN
MYSTERIES™

ANNIE'S
SECRETS
of the QUILT™

Chocolate
Shoppe
Mysteries™

SECRETS OF THE
CASTLETON
MANOR LIBRARY™

Visit us at AnniesFiction.com